CAPTIVE VOW

ALTA HENSLEY

Thank you to Pink Ink Designs for the photo, L. Woods PR for the cover design and PR & Mikey Lee for gracing the cover! Also a big thanks to Maggie Ryan for editing and helping my book turn to magic! I also can't forget Judy, Sandra, and Zoe for being exceptional betas! I have the best team in the world.

DEDICATION

To my readers.

The first ones, the current ones, and the future ones.

ALTA HENSLEY'S HOT, DARK & DIRTY NEWS

Do you want to hear about all my upcoming releases? Get free books? Get gifts and swag from all my author friends as well as from me? If so, then sign up for my newsletter!

http://www.subscribepage.com/i0n8g9

I take you.
To honor and obey.
Till death do us part.
This is my solemn vow.

I am caught in the madness of a deep obsession. Stolen away to become his perfect and dutiful wife. Trapped in a twisted and dark courtship. Forced and trained in the wifely duties of an obedient bride.
I am his.
Captive ever after...

***Captive Vow is a dark romantic thriller. If you don't like a sprinkle of shock, a dash of taboo, and a heavy dose of sex, then don't take a sip of my cocktail.

1

Jack and Jill went up the hill to fetch a pail of water.
Jack fell down and broke his crown,
And Jill came tumbling after.

My momma used to hum that nursery rhyme. She used to hum it a lot. And on days she was stressed, anxious, or short fused, she would even sing it with a high-pitched, haunting voice over and over again like a stuck record. It was the sound of my childhood. I hated that song.

I still remember the day I asked her why she loved it so. I wanted to know why two people climbing a hill and then falling off it was so important to her.

Who was Jack? Who was Jill? She had looked at me stunned, as if surprised I had noticed and had paid attention to her humming and singing it all these years. Or was she shocked I didn't know the answer to my question? Whatever it was, she studied me for several minutes before answering me.

"It was your father's and my song. It reflects us. Our love we once shared."

My mother never spoke of my father. I had never met him nor ever saw a picture. Whenever I asked about him, for stories describing who he was, my momma was quick to shut it down. She said he was 'gone' and that was the best answer I would ever get.

"A nursery rhyme?" I had asked. "*That* was your song?"

"Yes. It's about two lovers who beat all the odds holding them down. They climb above it all, but only to be crushed again."

"I don't understand. Why do they have a pail of water?"

"A pail of water is a euphemism for having sex. For finally being in love and able to be together. But then Jack dies... and Jill soon follows."

"They die?"

She nodded, appearing so deep in thought. "Yes, they both eventually die."

THE SOUND OF THE PHONE RINGING IN THE MIDDLE of the night was never a good thing. It's always the sound of bad news, an emergency, or even death. The shrill resonance cutting through the night's air is like a town crier announcing impending doom.

My heart thumped against my chest as I reached for my cell phone sitting on the nightstand beside my bed. The number on the screen showed unknown, which only intensified my panic.

I cleared my throat, not wanting to sound as if I had been woken from a deep slumber and answered, "Hello?"

There was an operator's voice on the other end. "This is a collect call for Demi Wayne from The Eastland Women's Correction Facility. Would you like to accept the charges?" I had heard this question many times before.

"Yes, I will accept the charges." I sat up in my bed

and turned on the bedside lamp, rubbing the sleep out of my eyes.

A clicking sound was followed by, "Demi?"

"Hello." I felt sick. I wanted to vomit. Her voice on the other end always made me feel ill, but tonight was worse. So much worse. I scanned my nightstand, wishing I still had the emergency pack of cigarettes I kept for an occasion such as this. Why the fuck did I decide to quit?

"How are you?" she asked.

What did she expect me to say? How was I supposed to be when I was getting a call from my mother in the middle of the night from a prison where she'd been incarcerated for the past six years? I needed a goddamn cigarette is how I was.

"Fine," I lied.

"Have you been watching the news?"

"No." Ever since my mother was arrested for blowing up a building and killing the five guards on that night's duty, I avoided the media completely. I couldn't take it. The pictures of her. The pictures of me. The pictures of us together and how the media would say I was a spitting image of my mother. They would say we looked like angels with our blonde hair and blue eyes, but then in the same sentence, say my mother had nothing but the devil inside of her. I didn't want to look like her. I didn't want to be the devil. I hated the media. I hated them all. I couldn't handle all the awful things being said about my mother.

Demon.

Murderer.

Monster.

And they were all true. Everything they said was true.

There was a long pause of silence. "I'm calling to say goodbye," she said with a wavering voice.

Bile built up in the back of my throat. "Goodbye?" We had already said our goodbyes when she was handcuffed and escorted off to prison. So what could she possibly mean by saying it again?

"I lost the final appeal."

I remained silent. I struggled to comprehend the information being fed through the phone line. It was as if my body was protecting me from processing the words threatening to shatter my soul. *Lost. Final.*

"I'm being sentenced to death tomorrow. Lethal injection. The lawyer says today was my final attempt at overturning the guilty verdict. I lost again."

Guilty.

The judge and jury had deemed her guilty.

She *was* guilty. She had placed the bomb in the building. She had killed those men. When she was asked why, she had said it was for the cause. The company housed in the building was testing against animals. *She* had been the judge and jury in that case, deciding that the experiments they were conducting deemed them worthy of being destroyed. 'A cause,' she had stated over and over. She was proud of her cause. She was proud of what she did. Not once did she say she was sorry. Not once did she glance over at the wives and families of the men she killed and beg for their forgiveness. Not once did she look at me and tell me she had made a huge mistake and wished she could take it all back. Not once did she show even an ounce of decency in her actions. When I had asked her why she would kill those innocent men, praying to God it was an accident, she simply shrugged and told me it was collateral damage. The price to pay for a bigger and better cause. So yes, what the media was saying about her was true.

Demon.

Murderer.

Monster.

My momma.

Yes.

So, I had no choice but to carry the shame for the both of us, and what a heavy weight it was. On my eighteenth birthday, I sat in the crowded courtroom and watched my mother stand with an aura of defiance and pride while the judge sentenced her to death for five counts of murder.

Happy Birthday to me.

"Demi?"

"Yes?" My voice cracked. I glanced around my bedroom at the piles of dirty clothes strewn about as my heart threatened to beat out of my chest. My room reflected my life. Dirty, neglected, disarrayed, shambles. My life was in chaos, and all I wanted right now was a fucking cigarette. This couldn't be real. This couldn't be real. This couldn't be real... yet, it was.

"Did you hear what I said?"

"Yes."

There was a long pause as darkness suffocated me. As darkness stabbed at my heart over and over. As darkness bludgeoned me to a bloody pulp. Darkness destroyed me as I sat there with the phone to my ear.

Dead man walking...

Correction.

Dead *woman* walking...

"It's okay, Demi. I'm at peace. I finally get to be with your father."

I said nothing as I struggled to breathe. The small room of my one-bedroom apartment shrank in size as the walls appeared to be closing in on me. I was trapped in this nightmare that I couldn't elude. There was no escape from my life.

"Jack and Jill went up the hill to fetch a pail of water. Jack fell down and broke his crown. And Jill came tumbling after," she sang softly as she had done so many times in my youth. She paused, as if she were waiting for me to say something. As if wanting me to ask for clarification.

I wanted to scream for her to stop. I didn't want to hear that awful nursery rhyme ever again. I wanted her to shut the fuck up! Yet, I didn't want those to be my last words to her. No matter what, she didn't deserve that. I didn't want her to die hearing my cruel—but honest—words ringing in her ears. A daughter's truth to a mother who had done her wrong... so very wrong. So, I remained silent. Silent like all the times I watched her and others meet in my living room planning to take down a government agency or corrupt company. These strangers plotting and planning in my childhood home all spoke as if they were the good guys, and everyone else were the villains. I had grown up to distrust our government due to all the conspiracy theories I heard growing up. I never questioned. I never disagreed. I never told a soul of their plans. I only remained silent as a good little girl would do.

"I'm proud. Your father died for his cause, and now I get to tumble down after him."

I had finally learned all about my father after my mother was arrested. Not from my momma, but by the television. The media had informed me that my father—who I was simply told was 'gone'—had died in a blaze of police gunfire when he refused to surrender after trying to blow up a nuclear power plant. He was a leader of a terrorist group. He had died that day, leaving behind a grieving widow and a three-month-old baby. I can still remember the news anchor who stared into the camera while video of my father played behind his profile. The anchorman's gray hair, perfect suit and blue-striped tie, his firm, emotionless expression as he spoke into the camera were still so clear in my memory. Did he know that behind his head on the television screen was a gruesome image playing of a man losing his life as he was gunned down? A man who was my father? Did the news anchor have any idea there was a young woman watching her father—who she knew nothing about—for the first time while he died on old video footage? I often wonder if that news anchor had any idea a piece of me died that day. I had to meet my father, watch them describe my mother as the devil, and come to terms with the fact that I was nothing but an orphan with a dark and twisted family tree. I was a fool. Fooled by my past.

"When?" I asked, swallowing the lump in the back of my throat. "When do you die?"

"They said two o'clock tomorrow."

Two o'clock.

Two o'clock and my mother would be dead.

How odd it must be to know the exact time you are going to die.

Was she afraid? I would be afraid.

The first hot tear fell from my eyes. "So this is it? The last time I get to talk to you?"

"Yes."

"Momma..." The rest of the tears followed as I slipped into a deep hole. At that moment, I wanted to be a little girl with her mother's soothing arms around her, comforting her, telling her it was all going to be okay. But nothing was going to be okay. Nothing at all.

"Promise me one thing," she said. "Promise me you'll find your Jack, and you will climb that hill. You deserve happiness and love. You deserve so much more than I was able to give you." She cleared her throat. "I have to go now."

Panic attacked. "Wait! Now?" Oh God! Was this the last time I would ever hear my mother's voice? Would these be our last words? "Is there anything we can do? Can we hold it off a little bit longer? Maybe hire another lawyer? Get a new judge? Anything? There has to be something!" I felt as if I was hanging on a cliff by my fingertips and the weight of my body was just too much. I was about to fall into the abyss.

"No. The time has finally come. Just know that though you may not have agreed with my cause or what I did, I at least stayed true to myself. True to what your father and I believed in. All I ask is you stay true to yourself, Demi."

"Momma..."

"Goodbye."

With a short metallic click, the phone went dead, and *Jill came tumbling after.*

2

Day of death. How do you start a day like that? Do you get up, shower, dress and go to work like any other day? How do you face the hours? The minutes? The seconds? How do you breathe when your soul is dying, but your body is too cruel to allow the sweet release of death? How does a daughter live as her mother prepares to die?

"Demi? Did you hear me?"

I turned to see Maria standing in the small break room, looking at me with concern. Her long black hair was set in a low bun like she always wore it while on shift, but the wayward hairs that framed her face revealed she had already worked several hours. The breakfast shift at *Blossoms Diner* could be a real bitch, and no doubt she was anxious to be relieved by me so she could go home and get some rest.

"What?" I hadn't even heard her come in, let alone say anything to me. Ever since the phone call, I felt as if I was wading through a dream cloaked in a thick fog.

"I asked if you were all right. You look a million miles away."

"Just a long night. I didn't get much sleep."

Maria was my friend—the only person I would really consider a friend—but I'd never told her about my mother. I hadn't told anyone about my mother. It wasn't exactly something I was proud of or wanted to relive by retelling the nightmare I tried desperately to keep locked away in the far corners of my mind. I had murderess blood that ran through my veins, and that was a secret I didn't want to reveal. Not to anyone.

Appearing satisfied with my lie, she said, "Story of my life. I swear, if Luis doesn't start sleeping through the night soon, I may die of sleep deprivation. He's just so darn cute that I can't help but pick him up from his crib. I know they say you are supposed to let them cry it out, but that just seems cruel to me."

I tried my best to give a smile and slight nod as I reached for my apron and tied it around my waist. Normally, I loved hearing stories of her sweet little baby, but the fog I was in nearly smothered me in despair. I was afraid Maria would know something was wrong by looking at me, as she always did. I just hoped today she'd write this one off as me being tired.

When I looked up at her after putting on my apron, I found her staring, appearing more concerned than before. "Hey, are you really okay? Are you sick or something? Do you want me to work your shift for you? I can call the sitter and have her stay longer. It's really not that big of a deal."

Having Maria work my shift would have been wonderful so I could just go crawl in bed and hide from all the emotions flooding me, but I didn't have the luxury. Missing even one shift meant me not being able to pay all my bills that month, and it was tight as it was.

I shook my head and gave the best reassuring smile I could give. "I'm fine. Once I get some coffee in me, I'll perk right up."

Maria seemed convinced with my answer, and she reached for the tie of her apron to remove it. "Table five is waiting for you."

"She's here today?"

"Every Tuesday and Thursday, and now Friday it seems. She's making a habit of eating here. Quite the regular. I already placed her order for her."

I let out a big sigh. Not that I minded our usual customer, in fact, she had become someone I actually cared for, but today I wasn't sure I had the patience or the ability to be kind to anyone. Viv Montgomery was a sweet old Asian lady with a heart of gold, but she did take a lot of my time and attention. "Any chance you can stay a bit longer? I know she'll need my help."

"Girl, you can't be expected to stop what you are doing and feed her every time she comes in."

Even though Maria said the words, I knew that if I didn't help Mrs. Montgomery eat her meal, Maria would most definitely step in and fill my shoes. She liked to play the hard ass, but I knew the real her. Maria wouldn't allow a little old lady to fend for herself, and I knew it.

Mrs. Montgomery had Parkinson's so bad, that bringing a spoon to her lips by herself, usually left her covered in whatever food she ordered. Seeing the poor woman sitting alone in the diner's booth, shaking and struggling a few weeks back, I had taken it upon myself to help her. It was the least I could do. And the truth of the matter was, I enjoyed it. I liked the lady, and I liked the feeling that I was being of some use to someone in need.

"Just stay long enough for me to get her started. Can you cover me?"

Maria nodded with a tender smile as she went to put her apron back on. "Softie."

"Yeah, I guess I am," I said as I reached for a ponytail holder in my pocket and pulled my hair into a messy bun, preparing for another long day on my feet serving greasy food to patrons. Hopefully, I would be busy enough to keep my mind off of the nightmare in which I was imprisoned.

When I walked into the dining room, I went straight to table five where Mrs. Montgomery sat staring ahead. Her short grey hair rested on the top of her shoulders, curled to perfection, with tiny, pearl pins right above her ears. It was still possible to see the remnants of what must have been rich black hair in her youth. In this redneck, piece of shit town in South Carolina, an exotic, mature, beauty such as Vivian Montgomery was a rarity. I had also come to realize that she dressed up for her special lunches each and every time. She treated lunch at *Blossoms Diner* like someone would treat a meal at a fine dining establishment. She always wore a dress or skirt, shoes with a stubby heel, nude-colored pantyhose, and carried a different purse that matched her outfit each and every time. She never wore garish jewelry, but she would wear a strand of pearls or a necklace made of some type of semi-precious stone. Though her hands were covered in age spots and wrinkles, her nails were always painted a pretty pink or coral, manicured to perfection. It was obvious the woman took pride in her appearance, and wanted to be at her very best, even if it was for lunch in a small local diner.

"Mrs. Montgomery, don't you look marvelous today," I said as I placed the Cajun chicken pasta she had already ordered from Maria in front of her shaking hands and sat in the booth opposite to her.

She looked at me with the sweetest eyes and the warmest smile. "You are so kind, dear." She reached across to touch my hands that rested on the table. I could see she was shaking more than normal. She had told me that, with her Parkinson's, she had good days and bad days, but by the intensity of the tremors now, I would say she was having a bad day. I noticed the skin around her wrists looked raw and bruised. So, I made a mental note to ask her about it later, but didn't want to start off the meal by talking about her sickness and injuries due to it. "You look so pretty too."

I smirked, feeling anything but pretty. I couldn't remember if I had brushed my hair. The fact that I was even dressed was a feat within itself.

"Don't give me that look," she playfully scolded. "When I was your age, I envied women like you. Tall, big blue eyes, long light hair, and the perfect cherub face. Like a doll. You are such a lovely young lady."

I smiled and shook my head, feeling uncomfortable hearing her kind words. I never handled compliments very well.

"Thank you," I mumbled as I glanced over at Maria who was taking an order at one of the tables I was supposed to cover myself.

Mrs. Montgomery looked down at her meal and reached for her fork. I always allowed her to start, judging if she needed my help or not. She always did, but I would still watch for a short time to gauge how much. Today she could barely grab the fork, knocking the other silverware to the side as she struggled for the handle of the utensil.

Without asking, I took the fork and poked it into a

piece of pasta and chicken. "Why don't I help you with that?"

She nodded and smiled. Her eyes made contact with mine, and we connected like we had done many times before. "Thank you. I don't know what I would do without you."

I fed her the food and returned the smile, poking the pasta for the second bite. "And I don't know what I would do without you, Mrs. Montgomery. You are the sunshine to my day."

"I wish you would call me Viv," she said as she finished the bite of her food. She then took another bite the minute she was done chewing, her entire body quivering lightly as she did so.

"I was taught by my momma to always address my elders in the proper fashion." I gave her a wink, trying to hide the stab in my heart which occurred by bringing up my mother.

Fuck! Why did I say that? I didn't want to think about her. I didn't want to remember a single thing. I just wanted to feed this nice woman and go about my day. One meal, one hour, one minute at a time, and I would survive this day. I had to survive the day my mother would die.

"You must have had a very good momma. She has

taught you to be a kind and generous woman." Mrs. Montgomery continued to eat, opening her mouth in a child-like fashion each time I brought the food to her lips.

A dull ache attacked my head, and a ringing filled my ears. I didn't want to talk about my momma. No, she was not a good momma. A good momma would not have done what she did. A good momma would not have left her child to fend off the cruel world by herself. A good momma would not die for a cause that did not matter. I did not have a good momma. I did not have a good momma at all.

"But I still wish you would call me Viv. Friends should be on a first name basis; don't you think?"

Trying to snap out of the spiraling fall from the cliff where I was so precariously balanced, I gave a smirk. "I suppose you are right. We are friends, and we should call each other by our first names. But that goes for you as well then. You call me Demi." She had only called me 'dear' since we first met.

Feeding Viv another bite, I noticed her eyes seemed to glisten as if she were struggling holding back tears. "I don't have any friends," she said.

"Oh, I'm sure you have friends."

She shook her head. "No."

I placed the fork down on the plate, reached for her glass of water, and helped her drink from it. "Well, I'll let you in on a little secret. Other than Maria who works here, I don't have any friends either. I pretty much keep to myself." I picked up the fork and once again stabbed at a piece of spiced chicken. "And the truth is, I often am suspicious of people who have lots and lots of friends. I mean, how can you be best friends with everyone? I think it's impossible. There's only so much of your heart you can give. I would much rather give more of me —the real me—to those select and special people than just a little of me to a large group simply so I can say I have a lot of friends."

Viv turned her head to look at Maria who was behind the counter getting drinks ready. "And Maria is your friend?" she asked.

"Yes. She's really nice and fun to work with. She has a new baby who is just about the cutest thing you've ever seen. We both don't have any family around, so we spend the holidays together... so, I guess you could say we are more than friends."

She looked surprised. "No family?"

I shook my head, hoping to God she would drop

the subject. I was not going to go into my awful situation with her or anyone. "No."

"And you don't have a special person in your life?" she asked as she reached for her napkin to wipe at some white cream sauce that stuck to the corner of her lip. Her hand shook the entire time, but she had managed to do it herself.

I shrugged. "Not interested in having a someone special right now."

"Why?"

I didn't usually like talking about myself to anyone, but this little old lady and I had spent many hours chatting as I fed her. I felt comfortable talking to her which was odd, but, at the same time, I liked it.

"All the good ones are taken, I guess." It was a canned answer, and one I really didn't mean. I had found it was a sufficient answer to give when people asked why you weren't in a relationship. It was a much better answer than 'I'm too fucked up to be with anyone.'

"Oh, I don't think so. You should meet my son. He's a good one. I raised him well." She smiled wide, intensifying the wrinkles at the corners of her eyes as her entire face seemed to light up. "But I could be biased since I am his momma."

"I didn't realize you had a son. You never mentioned him before." I had always gotten the impression Viv Montgomery was a widow and all alone. She had mentioned once that her husband had passed away many years ago, but that had been the only mention of family.

"I do. He's a handsome boy. He looks like his father did at his age. Thick black hair, hypnotizing brown eyes, firm jawline, muscular build. His Korean blood gives him a rich caramel-colored skin." She giggled. "Can you tell I am a proud mother? Yes, he looks just like his handsome father. My husband always had that powerful hold of my heart. Do you know what I'm talking about? That crazed, all-consuming love you can't live without." She paused, and a look of sadness washed over her face, but then was quickly replaced with a tender smile. "My son reminds me of him so much. Anyway, he's picking me up after my lunch today."

I tilted my head and studied her expression. I saw so much love and pride on her face. But if she truly loved and adored her son so much, why had she not mentioned him before? "I thought you took the bus here and home."

"I used to. But my son told me that, from now on,

he would be driving me to the places I needed to go. Such a kind boy."

"Does he live here in town?" I still found it odd Viv had never mentioned him before, and he was just now stepping in to care for her by providing transportation. I couldn't quite silence the warning bells going off in my head.

"Yes. He lives with me for now. He just returned, and it will take him a bit to get on his feet. But I'm in no rush for him to move out. I like having him around."

Ahh, a deadbeat son taking advantage of his mother is what this sounded like.

"What does he do for a living?"

"He's a pilot. He's loved planes from the time he could barely walk."

"You said he just returned. From where?"

Maybe I was being too nosy. But I heard the stories all the time of lazy and greedy family members taking advantage of their elders. I had no knowledge of Viv's financial situation other than the fact that she always paid in cash and would leave a very large tip. Sometimes too large, and she and I would argue about her overpaying me, but she always won out. I hated to think that her own flesh and blood could use her, or that anyone could take advantage of an elder, but I still found it a bit disturbing he was just *now* popping into her life. She had been coming here for months, me feeding her for an hour on those days, and not once did she mention any family at all.

Viv shifted in her seat, appearing uncomfortable. She didn't say anything, but rather opened her mouth to take another bite. I had overstepped it seemed.

"I'm sorry. I didn't mean to... I'm sorry. I'll mind my own business from now on."

Viv finished her bite. "Oh no. I don't mind. It's just hard to answer that question. I always worry he'll be judged and thought poorly of. He's such a decent and fine man, that it's a shame he has this mark on his past." She took a deep breath and continued chewing the food in her mouth.

Feeling guilty for doing exactly that—judging, I said, "Well, I'm the last person who has any business judging people. And we all have marks in our pasts. Some more than others."

Her tiny, frail body leaned inward. Lowering her voice, she asked, "You promise you won't think badly of him? He is such a good man. I would hate for you to think otherwise."

"If you say he is a good man, then I'll believe you." I gave her a reassuring smile. "I can't imagine you raising anyone but a fine, upstanding man anyway."

"He just got out of prison," she blurted, looking terrified the minute she said the words.

The word 'prison' hit too close to home, and I instantly felt sick to my stomach. I didn't want to think of prison. I didn't want to think...

"But he didn't do it!" she said in a hushed, yet aggressive tone. "He would never do the things they said. A man like my son would never kill a girl. They had it all wrong when they said he was guilty."

Prison.

Kill.

Guilty.

I couldn't cope. I couldn't hear these dark words that followed me wherever I went. Not today. Not today!

I put down the fork. "I really need to get to work,

Mrs. Montgomery. Maria is covering for me, but she really needs to get home to her baby."

Viv reached out a shaky hand to me. "Oh no. Please tell me I didn't scare you off with the news of my son. Please. I can see I have upset you. He was found guilty of manslaughter, not murder, but I swear to you, he didn't do it. And I feel awful now. I can see you are uncomfortable." She appeared to be broken-hearted, and I had never seen her so upset before.

"It's not that... I have a lot to deal with today." I struggled to hold back the tears threatening to fall. "It's not a very good day for me is all." I took her trembling hand and held it firmly. I wanted to reassure her that my demons were not due to her or the news of her son. My demons only needed the slightest push to be knocking at my door once again.

"I worry you are going to get up from here thinking my son is a bad person." Her lower lip began to quiver. "And he isn't. He really isn't."

I nodded and squeezed her hand again, not wanting my own morose thoughts to upset the woman. "I believe you, Viv. I do. I'm glad you have your son back." And I meant it. I'd always hated the thought of her having to deal with her illness all by herself. Now that her son was home, she wouldn't be alone. I scooted out of the booth and stood. "Bring him in next time, and I'll give him a free piece of Blossoms' famous cherry pie."

Her lip ceased trembling, a warm smile to replace it. "Oh I will. He would love that. You are such a kind girl. He will just adore you."

"Okay, well I really need to get to work," I said. "Are you coming in Tuesday?"

She nodded. "Of course." She clutched her hands together to her chest. "I can't wait for you two to meet. I promise you will see what a wonderful boy he is. He may be a bit of a momma's boy, but he is such a good, good boy."

3

I was in dire need of a cigarette. My body wasn't asking, but rather demanding I fill my lungs with the sweet and toxic smoke of nicotine. I shouldn't have stopped at the mini mart on the way to work, but I couldn't resist. I needed the security blanket. My intent wasn't really to smoke them... hell, who was I kidding? I damn well planned on smoking them. But fuck, out of all days, I would say I had a damn good excuse for cheating just this once. Knowing deep down I should simply ignore the craving and just relieve Maria so she could go home, I walked over to my friend, about to ask for another favor instead.

"I hate to ask you this," I began in a low voice by her ear. "Can you give me a couple of minutes to go smoke before you leave?" I hated myself for caving to my addiction, but I knew if I didn't get a smoke, I was going to snap at some poor unsuspecting customer.

Surprised, she looked up at me. "I thought you quit a few weeks ago."

"I did." I shrugged, feeling the shame of my nasty habit.

With skepticism in her eyes, she asked, "Are you sure everything is all right? You really don't seem yourself today." Maria knew how hard I had worked on quitting smoking, so this was a dead giveaway all was not well in the Demi Wayne world.

"I just got some bad news last night. But I really don't want to talk about it. At least not right now."

"Demi..."

"Please, I can't get into it here. I just need a little time to get my shit together. I'll be fine. I promise."

Was that a lie? I really wasn't sure. I was still walking. I was still going about my day. I was still breathing. So, I must be fine. Wasn't I?

She nodded. "Go ahead. I got this covered. Take as long as you need."

"Thank you," I said. "I won't be long."

I rushed out the back door and headed to the rear parking lot as I reached into the pocket of my apron like a junkie with shaky hands. By placing the pack of cigarettes and lighter in my apron before starting my shift, I had definitely set myself up for failure, since it was like a beacon leading me to the light. But my destiny to fuck up my nicotine-free life happened the minute the phone rang last night.

Correction.

It all started the minute my mother decided to kill those five innocent men, casting me into a fucked up nightmare.

Swallowing back my nausea, I came up with a plan. I was going to stand there, smoke, and not allow my mind to go to the dark place it wanted to go. It was 1:50. My mother would be alive for only ten minutes longer. She had ten minutes left to breathe the air on this earth as I stood in a parking lot behind an old local diner in a small deadbeat town polluting my own air. Fuck! Taking a deep drag, I silently cursed for allowing myself to think those thoughts. The only way I would survive this day was to go numb. I needed to go fucking numb!

Should I have been there? Should I have rushed to her side? But for what? To watch her die? I hadn't even visited her in jail once since the day we heard the words 'guilty.' I refused. For the first couple of years, I wouldn't even speak to her, or open her letters. I hated the woman who gave birth to me. I would never forgive her for choosing a stupid cause over her own daughter. I would never forgive her for loving a man who chose death over family. A man who I was forced to learn about on television. I would never forgive my mother. Never. But should I have made an exception today? Should I have been there?

Smoke. Just smoke. Nothing else. Mindless. Think of nothing.

I was losing my damn mind.

"Oh, dear. You should *not* be smoking. Those things are so bad for you," Viv Montgomery said as she walked up to me with a disapproving look. I hadn't seen her approaching me, or I would have tried to conceal the cigarette. I really didn't like anyone seeing me smoke.

I looked down at the lit cigarette in my hand with the smoke swirling around the tip. "I know. I've been trying to quit."

"Well, you share that curse with my son. I've been trying to get him to quit for years. But he's just so darn stubborn and refuses no matter how much I try to make him see reason."

"Momma! Come on! We need to get going." The deep, booming voice came from a large pickup truck that sat idling in the parking lot. There was a man standing by the open driver's door with a look of impatience on his face.

"That's my son," Viv said. She waved for her son to come over. "Pope, come meet my friend," she called out.

Hating I now had an audience watching me smoke, I dropped the cigarette to the ground and stomped out the flame with the sole of my shoe.

The man walked over with clenched fists, still leaving his truck running. "Momma, we need to go. I have someplace I need to be in ten minutes and still have to drop you off. I'm late."

As he got closer, I could see he was indeed the son of Viv Montgomery. Though she had claimed he was a spitting image of his father, I saw so much of Viv in his appearance. Dark hair, warm brown eyes, and a subtle Asian presence in his face. He was tall with broad shoulders, so clearly he didn't get his height and stature from his small-framed mother. He wore pressed khakis and a three-button black polo. His hair was slicked back, and he had nicely groomed facial hair. It couldn't be denied the man was extremely handsome. He was casual yet professional in appearance. Maybe he was heading to a business meeting since he was dressed nicer than any other man in this denim-wearing, cowboy boot-adorned town. If that were the case, and he was indeed late for a meeting, I would try my best to excuse his agitated demeanor. I didn't like to be late to things either.

"Let me introduce you to my friend first," Viv said. "Pope, please meet Demi. Demi, please meet my son, Pope."

I gave a weak smile. "Nice to meet you."

He didn't return the smile. If anything, he seemed to scowl before he looked at his mother with stern eyes. Ignoring me completely, he said, "We need to go, now."

A pinkish hue tinted Viv's olive-colored cheeks, as the quivers in her body seemed to intensify. "Oh, I..."

Her son was a rude bastard. All she wanted to do

was introduce us, and she had been so excited about it.

Clearly irritated, he grabbed Viv by the wrist, which made her flinch in pain. I glanced down at her raw and bruised flesh and remembered how I had seen the injury on her wrists earlier. Pope didn't seem to care, which made me want to kick him in the balls—hard. Now I wondered how she'd actually gotten those bruises and damaged skin. Did he have any part in it? Was it possible for a son to hurt his own mother? Was Viv Montgomery in danger, and should I make a call to Elder Protective Services?

Trying to not pick a battle that wasn't mine, I swallowed back all the words I truly wanted to spew. "Let me walk you to your truck," I said, managing to control my anger. I knew the last thing Viv would have wanted was for me to cause a scene, even though it took all my might not to.

"I have it handled," Pope snapped as he pulled his mother to his side, leading her away.

He didn't look at me at all which I suppose was a good thing. If he had, he would have seen my anger and distaste for him. Viv was a frail little old lady, and he was handling her like a criminal. Her tiny little body next to his much larger and muscled one were polar opposites. Strong versus weak. Young versus old. Bad versus good.

Viv looked over her shoulder at me with a worried look as she was led briskly to the truck. "Another time, dear. When my son doesn't have to be somewhere..."

I gave her a reassuring smile and lifted my hand to wave goodbye. Pope tugged her again, which forced her to look away from me. My heart went out to the woman. I knew her well enough to know she was embarrassed by her son's behavior—who wouldn't be—but I wasn't going to make her feel worse by appearing as if it had bothered me. At the very least, the asshole did assist her into his high truck by lifting her gently inside. Once he closed the door and walked around to his side of the vehicle, he did take a split second to glance at me and in that fleeting moment, we locked eyes. Hopping in, reversing the truck, Pope and Viv drove off, leaving me with a sick feeling in my stomach.

I needed another smoke. I knew it was bad, but I didn't actually get to finish the first one. Maria did say I could take my time, and I had covered for her many times in the past. However I wanted to justify it, once again, my body demanded I smoke another. I was weak, and my urge was strong.

Lighting up another cigarette, darkness knocked at my door. What time was it? What time was it? What time was it? Three gut wrenching knocks to my delicate psyche.

I glanced at my watch, not being able to resist. 1:59.

One minute left. My mother had one minute left.

What was she thinking? Was she scared? Was she crying? Was she finally having regrets? Was she thinking of me as I was thinking of her?

Thirty seconds...

Was there a heaven? A hell? Where would she go? Would she meet the devil himself?

Fifteen seconds...

Would the families of the murdered men get closure now? Could they heal as they all deserved to do?

Five seconds...

Would I survive this? Or was I doomed to be fucked up forever? Was it possible to find closure of my own?

Two o'clock. Death time. The end.

It was two o'clock and my mother was dead. Maybe not quite yet since I assumed the lethal injection took some time to work, but the end was now. No more appeals. No more waiting. My mother was dead.

The sound of crying surrounded me. A loud, all consuming wail ricocheted off the brick building of the diner and engulfed me in the miserable sound. I was on my knees, staring at the cigarette I had dropped, still burning on the asphalt.

Warm arms were around me, rocking me back and forth. "It's all right, Demi. I'm here. I'm here." Maria spoke the words. She was holding me. It was then that I realized those anguished howls were my own. I couldn't breathe as I cried into the shoulder of my friend. Over and over, she rocked me until she softly asked, "What's going on?"

I shook my head, not wanting to tell her the truth. What would she think? How could I even say the words? The fabric of her shirt was now soaked to her skin as I continued to sob. I couldn't stop, and I feared I never would.

"You're scaring me. Are you hurt?"

I shook my head again.

"Please tell me what I can do." The sound of desperation in her voice and the way she held me told me she cared. Maria truly cared.

"My mother," I began to confess, "is dead. She died." That was all I could say. Those words were enough. And as I hiccupped and choked on my own agony, Maria continued to rock me like a mother consoling her baby.

"I'm sorry," she whispered against my hair. "I'm here. I'm here."

Maybe it was an hour, or maybe it was five minutes. Time had no bearing in my grief. But finally my tears dried up, and my heart seemed to beat again. Pulling away from Maria's shoulder, I looked into her tear-filled eyes. "Thank you." I could see she was pained by my sorrow, and I knew she didn't have to be there for me. "Thank you," I repeated, not sure how to express what it meant to me that she was there.

She helped me up off the ground and wiped her hands on her apron. "Are you going to be okay?"

I nodded, though I had no idea what the true answer to that question really was.

"I want you to go home. I'm going to go back in and cover your shift." When I opened my mouth to argue, she raised her hand in the air. "Go home, Demi. You just lost your mother and are in no condition to work. I have this covered. Go home."

Feeling the wobble of my knees, I knew she was right. I'm sure I looked like a disaster with red, swollen eyes, and I seriously doubted I could speak more than a few coherent words at a time.

"Okay," I softly said. "Thank you." I appreciated she wasn't asking for details. She wasn't firing questions at me I didn't want to answer. I wasn't sure I could answer even if she did.

"I'll check on you after work."

"No, please. Get home to your baby. I'll be fine. I just want to close my eyes and escape the pain." I gave her a weak smile. "Or I'll run away and join the circus. Start a whole new life. One where I don't have to face my shitty past and present."

Maria smiled warmly and gave me a hug. "You better not leave. You owe me a shift trade now."

Enjoying the security of her arms around me, I whispered, "Thank you. You are a good friend."

She pulled away from the hug and wiped at the last tears on my cheeks with her fingertips. "I'm so sorry about your mother. I can see how much she meant to you. But right now you need to go home, take a sleeping pill, and face the new day tomorrow. You're strong. You got this."

I took a deep breath, happy I had Maria's strength to count on. "Okay. Thank you."

As she led me to the break room to get my stuff, she teased, "You would make an awful clown at a circus anyway. So I guess you are stuck at *Blossoms Diner* with me forever."

4

Two sleeping pills and two large glasses of wine to wash them down with, and my tiny couch was calling my name. I considered going straight to bed, but since it was still the middle of the day, the couch seemed less depressing. The light blue, rough-textured couch was actually the only piece of furniture which I owned that hadn't once belonged to someone else. Every piece of furniture scattered around my tiny apartment was either acquired from a second hand store, a garage sale, or given to me by someone who had bought something new and now considered their old piece of furniture trash. It wasn't like my couch was anything fancy. It was part of a Labor Day blow-out sale, and it had a small stain on the cushion, hence the extreme discount, but it was all mine, and it was new. And the day I purchased that luxury item was memorable. I had suddenly felt like an adult. As if buying a couch finally gave me the adult card that allowed me access into the special adult club. Growing up with few possessions, I was one who never gave value to things such as fancy furniture. But that little blue couch gave me a sense of comfort every single time I walked into my apartment. It stood out to me against my brown and dull carpet. It shined and sparkled in a white-walled room. It was mine. It was a symbol that I would emerge from whatever hole I felt trapped in. It promised a time when I would someday drag myself out of my self-imposed prison and find the normal I so desperately craved. A blue couch was normal, and I now had a tiny piece of it.

Normal.

Someday I would be normal.

But today was not that day...

So, all I had was my normal couch to count on now. I could lie under a thick blanket and drift away as I watched a mindless movie as normal people often do.

Stumbling my way over to the living room after putting on sweatpants and a white tank, feeling a bit light-headed, I realized I might had gone a bit overboard on drowning away my sorrows, but at the same time, I really didn't care. I was a fucking disaster. But I also think it was fair to say that anyone would have given me a free pass for being one.

There was a faint knock on the door and I paused, wondering if I was hearing things. My head was heavy, and I could barely keep my eyes open, so it was likely I could be hallucinating sounds too. There was another knock and then a third. It was too early for Maria to be stopping by and checking on me, so I questioned if I should even open it. Salesperson maybe? When the fourth knock came, I made my way to the door on shaky legs, feeling whoever this person on the other side was, wasn't going to go away until I answered.

Cracking the door open, I struggled to process why the little old lady was at my door. "Viv?" I opened the door the rest of the way. "What are you doing here?"

"I'm so sorry I dropped in unannounced like this. I wanted to come by and apologize for my son's behavior." She had her tiny hands clasped in front of her as she looked down at her feet. "May I come in?"

I stepped to the side and motioned for her to enter, too stunned to do anything else. "I'm confused. How did you know where I lived?"

She looked around the apartment—no doubt taking in my lack of decor—as she stood by the couch that was still calling my name. "I went back to the diner after my son dropped me off. I couldn't leave having you think ill of him. It killed me knowing you may think so." Her body shook as worry washed over her face.

It seemed odd Maria would have given her my address, especially knowing how upset I was. But maybe she thought Viv could help in cheering me up. "We all have our bad days. I'm sure he was just in a rush," I reassured her. "I hate being late for appointments too." I didn't mean any of what I said and still felt her son was an asshole, but if putting her mind at ease was what she needed, then I would.

She clapped her hands together. "Oh, I'm so happy you understand. Yes, he had an important business meeting. He's liquidating assets in a company he had a large stake in. He was..." she paused, looking pained by her thoughts, "he is a very successful and wealthy man. So sometimes work can be very demanding for him."

Figures. It seemed all wealthy men were assholes. At least the wealthy men I had encountered. Assholes. All assholes.

"I thought you said he was a pilot." My head swam with the booze and pills, and I worried that if I didn't sit down soon, I would collapse. So, I walked over to the couch and plopped down.

She looked down at me but remained standing. "Oh he is. As a hobby rather than a profession. He bought and sold companies before..."

"Before he went to prison," I finished for her, feeling it was always better to address the elephant in the room rather than skirting around it.

"Yes, before that."

Yawning big, I said, "To be honest, I didn't like watching him hurt you."

"He didn't hurt me," she defended. "Not at all."

I glanced at her damaged wrists. "He grabbed you." I pointed at her injuries. "How did you get those marks?"

She covered her wrists with each of her hands, trying to conceal what I could already see, and what I had already seen at the diner.

"Did he do that to you?" I asked, even though I was pretty sure I already knew the answer was yes. The look on her face and in her eyes revealed I was correct in my assumption.

"Not on purpose," she continued to defend. "It was because I tried to break free."

A thick fog of sleep was rolling in, so it was getting harder to comprehend the conversation. What she said made no sense to me. "What are you talking about? Break free?"

"Oh, it's complicated. It has to do with my condition. Just know my son is a good, good man."

Exhausted, and not feeling able nor wanting to discuss this any longer, I decided to table it for another day. "I'm sorry, Viv. I'm not feeling very well," I said as I rubbed my eyes with my hands. "I really need to get some sleep."

"Oh you poor dear," she said as she came to me and placed her soft hand on my forehead. "Do you have a fever?"

I shook my head. "I just need to sleep."

She glanced at the empty wine glass on the coffee table. "Let me get you a drink of water. I bet you're dehydrated. You sit right there." Without waiting for an answer, she walked over to the kitchen. I could hear a few cabinet doors open as she searched for where I kept my glasses, followed by the water running in the sink. A few moments later, she brought the glass of cool liquid to my lips, not giving me a choice but to drink from it. Her hands didn't tremble at all which was surprising considering how badly they had shaken earlier in the day.

"Thank you," I said, wanting to be polite but really wishing she would just leave me be so I could drift off into the abyss of sleep.

She forced me to drink some more. "This should make you feel all better." Looking at me with the most tender of eyes, she asked, "Is everything okay?"

Fresh tears began to well up, and my lip quivered as I said, "It's been a tough day." A warm tear fell down my cheek. "I just want to close my eyes, wake up tomorrow, and start a new day. A new life. A new everything."

She wiped at a falling tear with her tiny and frail hand. "I've often wanted to do that too. But it's not always that easy. Your demons always remain inside you, so no matter where you go, they go too. You have to learn to fight them off instead."

"They've won. There are more of them than me, and they have won." My words slurred together in one jumbled mess.

"No, dear. You are a strong woman. I can see that. You have such a wonderful life ahead of you. I know this with all my heart. You will find love and live happily ever after."

Giving up on fairytales years ago, I simply shook my head.

"You'll see," she reassured. "You'll wake up, and a brand new life will be waiting for you."

Finishing the last of the water, I rested my head against the pillow and closed my eyes. The pills were winning. "Viv, I'm really sorry for being so rude. I took some sleeping pills before you arrived, and I really need to just go to sleep. I appreciate you coming by, but would you mind coming back another time? Or maybe we can talk tomorrow at the diner." I hoped my words were more coherent to her than they sounded to me in my fuzzy head.

She reached for the blanket and covered me with it, tucking it under my chin. "I completely understand. But I insist on staying until you fall asleep. It's the least I can do for causing all the trouble today."

I didn't have the energy to argue with her, so I closed my eyes, nodded slightly, and snuggled into the blanket, ignoring the awkward fact that Viv stood over me, watching.

She was harmless.

Just there to help.

Being motherly... motherly. Like I knew what 'motherly' really meant.

Just as complete darkness was about to take hold, there was another knock at the door. Feeling like my head weighed a hundred pounds, I struggled to sit up. It was still way too early for Maria to be stopping by. Viv softly eased me back down, though I'm not sure I would have been able to stand up if she hadn't. I'd definitely overdone it on the booze and pills. I had no idea they would knock me out like this, and they seemed to grow in intensity with every second.

"I'll get it, dear. You just rest."

Lying back down, I wasn't going to argue. Not that I had much of a choice.

"What are you doing here?" Viv asked in a hushed voice to whomever was on the other side of the door. "You shouldn't be here yet. It's not time." I heard the closing of the door.

"Who was that?" I asked, struggling to push myself up so I could go see, but failing. Was it Pope coming to pick her up to take her home? I didn't like the idea of the man knowing where I lived.

"Nobody, dear," she said with a warm smile as she came back and adjusted the blanket on me again all nice and snug. "Don't bother yourself. I just shooed him away. I have it all under control. You just sleep."

"If that was Pope—"

"Oh, no. That wasn't Pope, dear. He doesn't know I'm here."

Why was she lying to me? Of course it was Pope. Who else would she be speaking to?

Who cares...

Feeling as if my body was being swallowed up by a big, thick, all encompassing black wave, I had no choice but to comply. Darkness equaled peace.

5

My mouth was dry—so dry—and my eyelids were still heavy as I struggled to pry them open. Waking from my drug-induced slumber wasn't coming easy, and I wondered if I could have overdosed on the sleeping pills and wine. Was I okay? Would I be able to wake up? Was I dying? Would booze and sleeping pills be the end of me? Why was it so hard to wake up?

Wait... I couldn't move...

I couldn't move! My eyes were open but everything was black. Blinking to make sure my eyes were really open, I saw absolutely nothing. Panic sunk in when I realized I couldn't move because I was tied up. My wrists were bound. My ankles were as well, and I was balled up and placed in something that prevented me from thrashing around. Was I in a box? I tried to scream, but a gag, stuffed between my lips and tied around my head, prevented anything other than a muffled whimper from coming out.

I struggled against the restraints and rocked my body against the walls of my tightly-confined prison. There was no room to do anything as my trapped body took up every last inch of space. I couldn't even stretch out my legs.

Oh God!

Fuck!

Please! Please! Please let this be a dream!

I screamed again, but any noise that did escape from my gagged mouth only bounced off the walls of my dark confinement. There was nothing I could do. I couldn't move. I couldn't see. I couldn't even cry for help.

How did this happen?

How did I get like this?

Who did this to me?

My last memory was falling asleep on the couch as Viv tucked me in...

Oh God, was Viv kidnapped too? Was she bound and gagged in a box as well? That poor old woman. She was too frail, too sick! She would die! Did the monster who did this know she would die?

I flung my shoulder into the wall of my prison, hoping I could somehow let someone know I was captive. I screamed, though again, it came out muffled. I gyrated my body with every ounce of strength I had as hot tears ran down my face, and then I stopped when I remembered the knock. There had been a knock on my door before I fell asleep. Viv knew the person...

Pope. Her son.

He did this! It was Pope Montgomery who had kidnapped me!

But why? Why would he do this? Because I was friends with his mother? It didn't make sense, but, then again, there's no sense in insanity. I did, however, have a small moment of relief knowing Viv was not also gagged and boxed like an animal. There was no way Pope could do something so awful to his own mother. But why me? Why would he do this?

I recalled the conversation I had with Viv in the diner. She had said her son went to prison. He was a criminal. Viv also had said he was a good man... But wouldn't any mother say that? Fuck! She said he went to prison for killing a girl. For killing a girl! Fuck!

"Help me!" I screamed against my gag. Pope Montgomery was going to kill me! "Help! Help! Help!" He was going to hurt me like he had done to the poor girl. He should have never been released from prison. Never! "Help me, please!" I sobbed as I gasped for air. I was going to die.

Whatever had been used to tie my wrists and ankles rubbed my flesh raw with every movement I made, and the breathable air of my tiny prison seemed to be growing thinner by the minute. My throat was so dry that my weak screams only made it worse. My fight was futile. The rational part of my brain told me I needed to remain calm and conserve my energy. There would be a moment when he would open the box. And in that moment, I would strike. I would give it all that I had. Even if he killed me, I would make sure my fucking DNA was all over his fucking face.

Breathe. Breathe. Breathe.

Wait. Wait. Wait.

Oh shit... what if Pope had buried me alive? What

if he was never coming back? What if this was where I would die? Is that why the air seemed thin? Was I buried alive?

Just as complete hysteria almost set in, I heard a loud sound outside the box. It sounded like a storage door was being lifted. Maybe? Could it be possible I was in a box in a storage unit?

A few moments later, someone was working on removing the top of my coffin. This was my chance. Fight or die. I swallowed back my fear the best I could and waited as rays of light entered my tomb as the lid was lifted. Now that the top was removed, I quickly glanced around and confirmed I was indeed tied with rope and trapped in a small wooden box. A crate similar to one you would use for transporting cargo. I was barefoot and still wearing my black sweats and white tank top from before this all happened. Squinting against the light, I saw an angel looking down upon me.

"Viv!" I desperately said against my gag. It was Viv, and she was there to help me.

She appeared so scared as she put her finger to her lips to signal my silence. Her eyes looked away from me and scanned the area as if she was waiting for Pope to arrive any minute. "Please be quiet," she whispered. "Don't let Pope hear you."

I did as she asked and didn't scream even though I wanted to. Her obvious fear of her son only made my own horror increase in magnitude. I couldn't figure out where we were. All I could see was what looked like a metal wall behind her.

"I brought you some water," she said as she revealed a plastic bottle in her shaky hand, "but you can't say anything. Please, don't say anything." She paused and looked down on me with pleading eyes.

I nodded, desperate for the water.

She reached into my box and pulled the gag away from my mouth, and then she put the bottle to my lips. I gulped the water down in big swallows, emptying it halfway before she pulled it away. There was a weird aftertaste, but I didn't mind since I couldn't remember ever being so thirsty.

"Viv, please," I whispered. "Help me get out of here."

She shook her head as the look of terror intensified in her eyes. "I can't. Not yet. You just have to be really quiet. He can't hear you, or he will end it. You don't want him to end it. I don't want him to end it!" Tears filled her brown eyes, and her bottom lip quivered. "Please trust me. I will get you out of here and keep you safe. But you have to trust me and not make a single sound."

"Untie me! Find something to cut the ropes. There's got to be something around that you can use."

She shook her head. "I can't."

"Yes, you can. Just look around and find something sharp. Hurry before he comes."

Her fearful eyes turned to ones of sadness. "I can't. You have to believe me. He won't understand."

"Viv, hurry!"

"I can't."

"Don't leave me in here. Untie me, and I will run as fast as I can. I won't tell anyone. I promise! I won't tell anyone about your son. He won't get into trouble. I swear." I would have told her anything, and I knew she was scared I would run to the authorities and have him arrested for kidnapping. I didn't want her maternal instincts to protect her son preventing her from helping me escape. "We can all pretend this never happened. Please."

She put the plastic bottle to my lips again and assisted me in swallowing the last of the water.

"We'll be there soon. When we get there, I will get you out of this box. I swear to you."

"Where are we going? What are you talking about? Where am I? Please, Viv. Tell me where I am. What's going on? What does he plan on doing with me? You have to help me. Please!"

"Shh... He can't hear you!" She hesitated and glanced around, appearing as if she was listening for any sound of Pope approaching. "You are in the back of a moving truck. You are hidden and safe. But we have to keep you hidden, so you can't make a single noise. We stopped for a break, but the next stop will be when we get there. And when we do, Pope and the movers will be here to move the box. But we *have* to keep you hidden! It's crucial or else. You have to stay quiet and remain perfectly still the next time the truck stops. You have to!"

"Viv, I know he is your son, but you can't allow him to do this to me. Please help me. I'm not asking you to call the police, but please help me out of here."

"I'm doing what's best. I know him. I know what he will do if he finds out I'm talking to you right now. So, you have to be quiet. You have to!"

A metallic taste coated the inside of my mouth and my head felt foggy. The water hadn't alleviated the rawness of my throat, and if anything, had intensified it. My eyelids threatened to close as my body seemed to melt into the bottom of the box. I was unable to feel the restraints digging into my skin—I couldn't feel much of anything any longer. I couldn't lift my arms or even wiggle my fingers. "The water," I mumbled. "What was in the water?" My eyes rolled to the back of my head as I struggled to keep my lids open.

"It will help you sleep. So you will be comfortable for the rest of the drive. I know this box is small, and I don't want you to panic. But I promise you, when we get there, I will make everything right. I will."

"Viv..."

"Just don't let him hear you. You have to trust me. I know my son. You can't let him hear you."

She put the gag back around my mouth. I couldn't resist even though my soul was screaming in desperation as darkness once again took over.

6

Waking up again was a repeat of the most horrid nightmare of when I'd awoken before. I was on a sick merry-go-round in the depths of hell. My hands were still tied, but my mouth was no longer gagged, and I was sitting up, strapped to a wooden chair. Lifting my head that rested limply on my chest, I took in my surroundings with blurry eyes. I was in a basement or wine cellar. There were boxes all around me, and to my right and left were shelves that housed dusty bottles of wine. The room was dark, dank, and there was a sharp chill in the air. In front of where I sat was a staircase leading to the floor above.

Pulling against the straps that held me securely to the chair, I wasn't surprised I couldn't make them budge. Pope wasn't going to lose his captive because of loose knots. He clearly was a pro at this. Taking a deep breath, I struggled with the battle going on inside of me. I was at war with the frightened little girl who wanted to scream for help. This little girl psyche was pleading and begging I do something—anything. But I remembered what Viv had said. How it was important for me to remain silent. She said she would help me. But I wanted to scream at the top of my lungs more than I wanted to even breathe.

Where was Viv? Where was she?

Where was Pope?

Where was I?

"Oh good. You are awake," came Viv's gentle voice behind me.

I tried to turn to see her, but was unable to. All I could see were stacked boxes all around. "Viv? Hurry, untie me."

There was silence.

I wiggled my fingers and toes and was pleased I

still had feeling in them. I would at least be able to run once I was free.

"Viv?" Why wasn't she rushing to me to free me from my restraints? "We need to hurry."

Silence.

"Viv!" I wiggled in my chair as if showing her that I was tied and couldn't move would trigger her to take action. "You have to do something before Pope comes back down here. Please hurry."

"Now, Demi. The more you resist, the more those ropes are going to flaw your perfectly creamy skin." I froze in place as a chill ran down my spine. The voice was Viv's, yet it wasn't Viv's. She had a thick southern accent that seemed to ooze off her tongue. It reminded me of a southern belle attending charm school so she could win the local beauty pageant. "It's important you take care of your skin, child. No man wants a woman with raw and red wrists and ankles. It simply isn't ladylike. You must remember that."

The click of heels on the cold concrete floor came from behind until they circled around and stood before me. Viv Montgomery stood before me. The sweet little old lady whom I had fed in the diner because she wasn't able to feed herself, stood before me. Yet, this person wasn't Viv. This woman seemed different. It wasn't just her thick southern accent that I had never known Viv to have, it was something more. This woman stood with a straight back. Her chin lifted with a sense of arrogance mixed with elegance. There was no shaking or even a tremble of a single body part. She was composed and exuded a sense of strength. She wore a wool, cream pencil skirt, a perfectly pressed ivory blouse, and her trademark tan pantyhose that I recognized. Yet this was not the frail, Asian lady who had Parkinson's that I knew. This woman even appeared younger in age if that were possible, and definitely much healthier.

"Viv?"

The woman frowned. "Don't ever call me by that. Vivian Montgomery is my name. I do so hate when people use nicknames. If your parents had intended for you to be called by your nickname, then they would have named you as such. I was not named 'Viv,' therefore, do not call me that." She cleared her throat and clasped her hands neatly in front of her. "You may, however, call me Vivian. I usually require younger folk to call me Mrs. Montgomery, but since you will soon be family, I will allow you to call me Vivian. Once you are married to my son, we can then discuss the possibility of you calling me Momma." She smiled as her eyes seemed to drift off in thought. "I've never had a daughter before, and I might quite enjoy it."

I sat dumbfounded. Who was this person? Why did she suddenly have an accent? What was she talking about? Marrying her son? *Momma*?

"What's going on? You said you would help me escape when we got here." I looked around, still having no idea where 'here' even was.

With a smile that reminded me of one the devil himself would have painted on his face, she said, "Correction, child. I told you I would make everything right. I never said I would help you *escape*." She walked up to me and moved a piece of wayward hair that had fallen in front of my eyes and gently tucked it behind my ear. "And there is absolutely nothing to *escape* from."

My inner little girl who had been pounding on my chest in panic finally won. I started to cry and shake in fear. "Why are you talking like that?"

"Like what?"

"That accent."

"Accent?" She giggled. "Well, child, we do live in the South. And besides, if you ask me, it's those Yankees who have the accent. Why are you asking such a funny question?"

Had Viv been lying to me the entire time? Had she pretended to be sick to trap me? Was this some cruel game she and her son played with unsuspecting women? Had I been fooled all this time, and now I was going to be murdered because of my naiveté?

"I just want to go home," I sobbed. "Please, I don't want any trouble. Just let me go, and we can pretend none of this ever happened. I won't say a single word to anyone. I promise."

Her eyes widened and her eyebrows rose. "Home? Child, this is your home. Your *new* home. Pope bought this house years ago to be used for vacation. As lovely as it is with all the trees and mountains surrounding us, it was simply too impractical to reside here full-time. Well, with Pope's job and all. But now that he is retired, it really is the perfect place to live." She began to pace a little as she spoke. "At first, it was too far removed for my tastes. No town nearby, and the only way to get supplies is via plane. But since Pope is a pilot and we have a plane, and even one of those fancy landing strips, I guess we are some of the lucky few in the world who can live out here by ourselves."

"Viv, listen—"

"Vivian!" she snapped as she spun on her heels, her eyes shooting daggers at me. I flinched at the harshness, shocked to hear such venom come from a woman I once felt incapable of ever raising her voice. "You will call me Vivian. Do not make me tell you again."

I sniffed back my tears and struggled to regain composure. "I'm sorry. Vivian."

She smiled and softened her features again, yet she was still not the woman I had known before. "Now, as I was saying, child. Pope has worked hard all his life to provide for us. This house may not be in the ideal location for two women such as you and I who do sometimes partake in the social life, but we must see this as a wonderful opportunity. It will give you and me the chance to form a proper mother/daughter relationship, and allow you and Pope to take your time with your courtship. Young folk these days just don't court like we used to in my time."

Bile formed in the back of my throat. My head spun as my heart thumped against my breastbone. "Where am I?" My voice cracked as I trembled harder than the woman ever had in the diner.

"Deep in the woods of the Sierra mountains. The land has been in our family—on his daddy's side—for many years, but nothing was done with it until Pope. He built a glorious two-story house. There's a wrap-around porch just like I had as a child. He even added some rocking chairs to remind me of those days." Pride beamed from the woman as she gushed like nothing was out of the ordinary. As if there wasn't a tied woman sitting right the fuck in front of her!

"Vivian," I swallowed back my fear and tried to regain my composure the best I could, "why am I here?"

Her eyes widened, and she tilted her head. "Well, to marry my boy of course. What a silly question."

"You kidnapped me to marry Pope?" My head pounded and my heart threatened to jump right out of my chest. The drugs from the water still blurred my thoughts so the insanity of this situation couldn't fully set in. What the fuck was going on?

"Kidnapped? No, of course I didn't kidnap you." She began pacing again, each click of her heels setting a loud staccato rhythm.

"I'm tied to a chair. You drugged me." I wasn't sure why I had to state the obvious, but the woman appeared to not notice she had a woman bound to a chair in a cellar before her.

She smiled. "Well, yes. I suppose I did drug you. But a momma has to do what a momma has to do sometimes. I knew once I got you here, all would be just fine. Yes, just fine." Walking toward me, she once again reached for my hair and ran her fingers through the tangles. "Now that you are here, we can begin."

I scrutinized her eyes. The same eyes that I had looked into so many times as she shook so hard before me that she was unable to even lift a fork. "Begin? Begin what?"

"Well, we have to teach you the ways of a proper wife. It takes training to be a good wife. To be the kind of woman my boy deserves." She patted me on the head. "But don't you worry. Lucky for you, I'm a mighty fine teacher." She paused and took a few steps back and then clasped her hands in front of her, giving off a prim and proper aura. "I don't always have the best patience, but I have no doubt you will be a quick study."

"Where's Pope?"

She looked up as if listening for him. "He and the movers just got done unloading the plane. So now Pope is flying them back to the airport. It won't take long for him to return. It was so nice for the boys to be willing to help us get all our possessions here. And we had to have a few months of supplies as well. Even with the plane, it doesn't make sense to fly into town often if we don't have to."

The way Vivian spoke to me was as if nothing was wrong. As if I weren't kidnapped, tied to a chair, begging for answers. She spoke as if it was simply another ordinary day. Had she lost her mind? She clearly wasn't all there. She was a mad woman, and yet, how did I not notice this before?

"Please, let me go. Please." My voice was so weak that I wondered if she even heard me since she didn't respond for several moments.

"There's going to be a lot of work to do once Pope returns. We have to work extra hard at making this house a home. It's been neglected and requires some construction." She smiled and clapped her hands. "But the good news is, Pope is handy with the tools. He is such a man. He knows how to build and fix things like a proper gentleman. You will be lucky to have him as your husband. Not all men are good with their hands. But Pope is. He's a true man."

"Vivian, please listen to me." I swallowed hard and took a deep breath. "You don't have to keep me here. You don't have to. Untie me, and I'll run. You can tell Pope I got away, and you couldn't stop me. He won't blame you. It won't be your fault. And like I said, I won't tell anyone. I just want to be free. We can all pretend this was a big misunderstanding."

A look of confusion washed over her. "Now, why would I do such a thing, child? After all the work and months of planning to get you here? Oh gracious no. Getting hold of the drugs to put in your water in the apartment and then again in the box was hard enough. I was simply terrified I would kill you, especially when you muddled my plan by drinking wine and taking sleeping pills." She played with the pearls around her neck nervously. "I was so worried you had messed up all my planning. But we were leaving for the airport to fly to the Sierra mountains that afternoon, so I had no choice. I had to act then."

"You drugged me?"

"Well, I had to. I do hope you understand. It was to ensure your trip was more comfortable. I had your comfort in my thoughts at all times. I truly did. And when he put you in the box, I told him to be very careful. I didn't want your perfect little body all bruised. No man wants a woman with flaws on her body. No man indeed."

"You helped Pope put me in a box?" How could I have been fooled by this woman for so long? I had trusted her. I didn't think she was capable of hurting anyone. Fresh tears pooled when it became very clear that the little old lady I had grown to care for was in on this plan with her son to kidnap me the entire time.

"Oh Pope didn't put you in a box, child. He's a true gentleman and wouldn't partake in such an act. So I had Richard do it."

Shaking my head as if that would help make sense of this entire situation, I closed my eyes in hope I would wake up from this nightmare. "Richard?"

"Yes, Richard. He's such a nice man. I hired him several years back to be my handyman while Pope was in prison. He eventually became a caretaker and a friend of mine. Anyway, he will do just about anything I ask of him. He's a little slow," she pointed to her head, "in the mind, but he loves me so. I'll miss him, and it was a shame to see him leave on the plane with Pope to go back to the airport, but he has a bigger and more important job to focus on now."

Remembering the knock on the door in my apartment, it was starting to come together. "Richard came to my apartment to help you kidnap me?"

"I do wish you would stop using the term 'kidnap.' It sounds so torrid." Vivian walked over to a box and began searching the contents inside. "But yes, Richard helps me do whatever I need. In fact, he is helping you as well, so you should be grateful."

"Helping me?"

I could hear items in the box shifting about as Vivian dug around. "He's watching over your little Mexican friend and her baby."

Fresh fear punched me in the gut. "Maria? What are you doing with Maria and Luis?"

She stood up with scissors she had found in the box. "Nothing at all... yet. But that's up to you, of course. Richard is simply there to watch them in their day-to-day life. Unless, of course, I give him reason to do something else."

She approached me again, carrying the scissors as one would carry a dagger. I watched the shears and wondered if this was the tool that would be used to kill me. Was talking time over, and death time next?

Vivian rested the scissors on my shoulder. The cool metal sent a shiver down my spine. "It's a win-win situation for all," she began as she caressed the skin along my collarbone with the scissors. "Richard will make sure that woman and her baby stay nice and safe. I will make sure you stay nice and safe. That is, however, if you remain a good girl. As long as you don't give Richard or myself any reason to punish you, and then to punish Maria and that cute little infant of hers." She opened the scissors, placed the strap of my white tank top between the metal blades, and cut the fabric in half. "If you are good, then all is good in the world."

Maria and Luis! No!

"What are you doing?" I asked as she began cutting the shirt. As she mastered the scissors, I noticed her hands didn't tremble once.

"Child, we have to get you presentable. No proper lady wears attire such as this. And you really are in need of a bath. We can't have Pope seeing you in this condition, and he will be home soon. You must try to always be desirable for him at all times. It's important for a healthy sex life. And for a successful marriage, you must have a healthy sex life. You don't want his eyes wandering to another. Men are weak, but women are stronger. And if we focus on what makes a man tick, we can prevent such a distasteful act as cheating."

She continued to cut the ribbed fabric of my tank until it dropped off of me, completely baring my upper half. The cool air of the room hit my nipples, and the reality of what was truly happening began to set in. She then moved the scissors to my sweats and hacked away. The sound of shears slicing fabric echoed off the walls of my prison. I sat in shock as a woman cut my clothing off of me, and there was nothing I could do. I didn't even resist— not that I could have since the ties were still so tight around my wrists and ankles.

When she finally removed everything except for my pink cotton panties, I pleaded again. "Please, Viv... Vivian. Please don't do this. We were friends. Remember? We were friends!"

She brought the tip of the scissors to the edge of my panties and sliced through them effortlessly. "Which is why I chose you, child. You will be the perfect daughter-in-law. I knew the minute I saw you that you would be the perfect wife for my son. I just knew it."

She tugged at the fabric that concealed all that was left of my modesty and added the piece of material to the pile of my shredded clothing. I sat completely nude. Since my arms were tied behind my back, the position forced my breasts forward, putting them on full display. My legs were opened wide since each ankle was tied to opposite sides of the chair. I had never before felt more exposed and vulnerable.

Vivian gathered the pile of ruined clothes and then stood before me. Her eyes scanned my body from head to toe, and then from toe to head. "Yes, I chose correctly. I knew you would be a pretty thing beneath all those awful and unladylike clothes you wore. I simply knew it." She smiled and obviously was proud of what she saw as her chin lifted and her shoulders squared. "Yes, indeed. Pope is going to be very satisfied with what you have to offer. Very satisfied indeed."

She turned and made her way to the stairs leading to the upper level.

"Wait! Where are you going?" Panic attacked my core even more at the thought of being left tied to a chair naked by myself.

"I'm going to go get some warm water and a rag. It's time for your bath, child."

She continued climbing the stairs until she was completely out of sight. I then heard the sound of a door closing and the click of a lock.

7

I had never believed in God. Religion just wasn't something I cared to invest any energy in. But right now, you sure as fuck better believe I would pray to anyone who was listening. Struggling against my ties again, I tried to see if I could make them budge even a little.

"Fuck!" I screamed, though I knew no one would listen or care. There was no escape. I was defenseless and in the hands of a deranged woman and her crazy son.

I needed my survival skills to kick in. I had watched movies and had read books. The women who survived situations like this were strong and resourceful. They didn't cry and babble like a baby. They remained focused and always outsmarted the captor. But as tears ran down my face, and every single breath heaved from my chest, I knew that was all fiction. Fucking fiction!

No.

I needed to be strong. Strong.

Taking a deep breath, I decided to think about everything Vivian had said. There was another man helping them named Richard. He was on order to watch over Maria and Luis and hurt them if I did anything wrong, so I had to be extra careful. Two other lives were at stake beside my own. Vivian was smart—a complete whack job—but smart. She had been staking me out for months. She had to have known I had no one in my life besides Maria and Luis. My only weakness was those two innocent people who wouldn't hurt a fly. They didn't deserve this. I didn't deserve this! Vivian had to know how sweet Maria was if she had truly been planning this for months. But where did Pope fall in this plan? Why was he new to the stake out? How had I missed him this entire time? Had he truly been in jail up until now? Could they have masterminded this plan while he was behind bars so that he would have a woman at his mercy when he was free?

My body trembled out of fear but also from the

cold. Being completely naked in the bitterly cold cellar chilled me to the bone. My teeth began to chatter, and there was nothing I could do to warm my body. But I needed to focus. Focus.

Remembering Vivian's words, I continued to put together that I was in a home out in the middle of nowhere. I had been drugged, stuffed in a moving crate, transported by U-Haul to a plane, and then flown to this vacation home. So now what? She said she wanted to train me. I wondered if she was planning to keep me tied to a chair the entire time. Would this cellar be my permanent prison? Looking around again, I didn't see any windows or a way to escape. And even if I did, if this house was truly out in the middle of the woods only reachable by plane, where would I go? Vivian and Pope had clearly planned everything out perfectly. They even had an accomplice. This was not a rushed job done on impulse. This was executed exactly as they had planned. I was their victim, and it was clear this mother and son duo had preyed on me for a very long time.

"Demi?"

I looked toward the stairs, preparing for the worst. It was Vivian, but she sounded different.

"Demi? Are you down there?" The voice had no

accent. It was the same voice I had grown to care for over the past several months. It was the voice that belonged to the little old lady I had considered a friend.

"Viv?" I squeaked, not knowing what to say or what to think. I was scared I was imagining the nicer version of Vivian in a desperate need for hope.

The woman descended the stairs and rushed toward me. Her eyes were wide, and her entire body trembled. Her lips quivered so much that her speech came out stuttered. "Are you all right? Oh lord. Oh lord." There wasn't the slightest hint of southern accent in her panicked voice. This woman was completely different to the one who just cut all my clothing off of me and revealed her maniacal plan as if it were something completely normal.

"Help me! Untie me!" I wiggled against the restraints, hoping to God that Viv would finally come to her senses. I didn't have time to figure out what the hell was going on. I just needed to get her to free me before her mind flipped back to the southern belle from hell.

She looked at my naked body in horror as if she hadn't seen it before. "Oh no, no, no, no. This can't be happening." She closed her eyes and covered her ears with her shaky hands. "No, no, no, no!"

The sound of an engine in the distance outside caught both of our attention. Pope was landing the plane. I could hear it faintly outside the walls of my dark cell. I was frantic. I had to get free before Pope came down here. "Please! Viv, untie me. He's here. Please!"

She looked up at the ceiling as if she could somehow see a plane descending from the sky with her son in the cockpit. "Pope is going to be so mad! He's going to be so angry!" Her body shook so hard that I wondered if she would fall over. "Oh, I have no idea what he's going to do. He's going to be furious. So very, very furious."

"The scissors!" I tilted my head to where they rested on the top of a box. "Grab the scissors, and cut me free. Hurry! We don't have long."

Viv started hitting her skull repeatedly as she screamed, "Please stop! Please stop!" She continued to pummel her head with her tiny fists. The insanity before me only fueled my desperation more. "Please stop! Stop! Stop!"

"Viv! Hurry!" I shook my body against my restraints as much as I could to try to get her attention. "You need to calm down. Look at me, Viv. Look at me! Untie me now."

She finally stopped punching herself and froze for several seconds before lifting her head and staring at me squarely. And right before my eyes, she changed.

Her posture changed. Her shoulders squared. Her chin lifted. Her warm brown eyes darkened.

When she opened her mouth to speak, bile coated the back of my throat. "Calm down, child. You don't want to damage your perfectly creamy skin. Men don't like a flawed woman."

The sickly-sweet southern drawl had returned.

Vivian had returned.

"What the fuck is going on? Who are you?" I screamed at her. "Why are you doing this? Why are you acting like two different people?"

Vomit threatened to explode from my body. I had never seen or heard such a thing. It was as if a demon had entered Viv's frail little frame. The demon was Vivian.

"Who are you? What is this?" I screamed again. I screamed at the top of my lungs. I didn't care if Pope heard me. I didn't care who heard me. I had no control over my blood-curdling scream. I was terrified. I was sitting helplessly before the devil himself. I screamed again and again as the shrill sound of my howl rattled against my brain.

"Shut your mouth, girl!" Vivian snapped, rushing to cover my mouth with her hand that no longer trembled as it had minutes before. "He'll hear you!"

I continued to scream, her hand doing very little to conceal the sounds of my horror. Over and over, I screamed in desperation, in fear, and in realization that there was no escape from this insanity. This complete madness.

She pulled her hand away from my mouth and slapped me hard against my cheek. "I said be quiet!"

I stopped screaming, stunned from the blow. The momentary pause was just enough for me to hear the heavy boots of a man running toward the door that led to my hell. Pope was coming. He was coming. He heard my screams, and now hell would have to be paid.

Vivian looked over her shoulder as she heard the click of the cellar door opening. "You fool," she spat in a hushed voice. "You fool!"

"Momma! Momma! Are you okay?" The man sounded terrified, as if it were his mother screaming rather than me.

"Yes, Pope. I'm fine. I'm coming up there. Don't come down. I'm fine." Again, the accent was gone.

She rushed to the edge of the stairs to try to prevent him from walking all the way down, but it was too late. Taking the final step, his head turned and our eyes made contact. I was staring into the eyes of the ultimate demon. I didn't scream. I didn't cry. I simply sat there and awaited my death. Death was dressed in a black shirt, black pants, and black boots. Death was all black as he should be.

He was the first to break our stare. His gaze went from my eyes to my breasts—my nipples hard from the cold air—and then to my exposed sex spread wide before him. His look was not carnal in nature or lust-filled. Instead, it was one of surprise and even disgust. He then looked at his mother who stood there wringing her hands together in worry.

"Momma..." The way he said her name reminded me of the sound of when a bullet leaves a gun.

"Oh, Pope. Let me explain. I don't know what happened." The southern accent was still gone, and the slight trembles to Viv's body had returned.

If I wasn't sitting there watching it myself, I would have never believed it. The woman was morphing in front of me from one person to the next. Everything changed. Her voice, her attitude, and in many ways, her appearance as well.

"Fuck!" he thundered as he kicked a moving box that sat toward his right with a force that sent the box sailing through the air. "Fuck! Fuck! Fuck!" The deep baritone of his booming voice reverberated off the concrete walls and floor. "What the hell did you do? What did you do?" He ran his hand through his hair and then punched another box repeatedly as he roared like a beast.

I watched as Viv stood there in absolute panic. She glanced at me and then at him as he attacked the box with his fists with a vengeance. He finally stopped and spotted the scissors still resting on top of another box. Storming over to where they sat, he picked them up and came straight for me.

I flinched and prepared for the worst. "Please don't hurt me."

Viv didn't move to protect me as I had hoped she would. I don't know why I expected her to, but I did. I knew Vivian wouldn't, but I really thought Viv would.

Pope kneeled down before me—his face inches from my bare pussy—and brought the scissors to the binds wrapped around my right leg and proceeded to cut the rope. I watched him in disbelief, unsure of what his actions meant. He wasn't hurting me, and, in fact, was being gentle in the way he handled my leg as he held me steady to cut through the thick material of the rope. When one limb was free, he moved to the other ankle. Having my leg free, I thought about kicking him in the teeth, but reason won out. I knew I would lose that battle and only anger him more. I closed my legs, though, so as not to show the inside of my pussy any longer. He glanced up and noticed that I had done so. It was then that I felt humiliation for the first time. Fear was a much more powerful feeling than humiliation, so not once had I felt the heat of embarrassment reach my face... not until that very moment. Pope Montgomery had seen every inch of my body. No doubt with my legs spread as wide as they were, he had seen the lips of my pussy stretched open and even my clit. I had been on full display for him. But even being as close as he was to me, he never once touched me in a sexual manner nor even looked at me in that way. The confusion over this only intensified my fear. I had no idea what was going on, or what to expect.

When Pope freed my other ankle, he silently got up and worked on the bonds around my wrists. I stared at Viv who shifted her weight from one foot to the other, clearly worried about what Pope would do. Was she waiting for him to kill me? Would he have sex with me first? Was that the reason why he was freeing me?

The minute my hands were free, I covered my breasts and tried to conceal my body as much as I could. I remained in the chair even though part of me demanded I get up and run. But I also knew there was no place to run to, and, even if I tried, I wasn't stupid enough to think I could outrun Pope. One look at the man would tell anyone that he was in prime physical shape.

He walked in front of me and lifted his shirt above his head.

Fuck! He was getting naked! To have sex!

Not saying a word, he removed his shirt and put it over my head, then tugged it down, helping the fabric cover my body. His eyes made contact with mine, and I saw something different. The rage and fury I had seen earlier were gone. I couldn't exactly figure out what I saw, but it was different. He stood up, placed his hands on his hips, and simply stared at my balled up self. His muscled chest before me reminded me of a gladiator in some blockbuster movie. Every curve seemed to be enhanced by the rippled contours of his physique. I expected to see tattoos—most likely because he was in prison and I had always assumed inmates had tattoos—but there were none that I could see.

Pulling my knees as closely to my chest as possible, I asked in a weak voice, "What are you going to do to me?"

He looked at his mother. "How could you do this? How?"

Her mouth opened and then closed.

"After everything," he said with sadness lacing his voice. "After everything. How?"

"Pope, I tried. I tried!"

He shook his head, turned to look at me, and slowly extended his hand. "I'm Pope Montgomery. I promise you I will not hurt you in any way. You're safe."

I stared at his hand in disbelief and then back into his eyes. *Safe?* How the fuck was I safe?

When I didn't reach out to take his hand, he pulled it away just as slowly as he had offered it. "What's your name?"

I refused to answer. What the fuck was going on? Why was he acting like he didn't know who I was? Like he had no idea I was even down in his cellar tied up? He looked over his shoulder at his mother for the answer.

"Her name's Demi, remember? She's the girl from the diner."

It was then that he seemed to recognize me.

"What's going on? Who are you people?" I couldn't take it any longer. I had no idea what was happening. This multiple personality thing by the both of them was as disconcerting as it was disgusting. "Are you both trying to fuck with my head before you rape and kill me?"

"We aren't going to rape or kill you," Pope said calmly.

"Then what? What is it you want? Why did you kidnap me? To be your wife?"

Pope appeared as if my words stung. The perplexed look on his face only added to the insanity of my out of control nightmare. Why was he acting confused?

"My wife? What are you talking about?"

"Your wife!" I shouted as hysteria took over. "Your

mother told me she was going to train me to be your wife! What kind of sick people are you?"

Pope walked over to his mother and grabbed her by her upper arms. "Momma, you tell me right now what is going on. Why did you do this?"

Viv shook her head. "I tried to stop her. I tried so hard! But she's stronger than me. She has all the control when she wants it. I couldn't stop it."

Pope released his grip, and his head sunk to his chest as he closed his eyes and took a deep breath. My body shook beneath the warmth of his cotton shirt that thankfully was large enough to cover most of my body as I waited for either one of them to explain what was happening. I was in the most fucked up episode of *The Twilight Zone*.

"I'm sorry, son. I am. It was out of my control."

He finally looked up with glassy eyes, didn't respond or acknowledge his mother, and then walked over to me. "Let's get you out of here." Without asking, he bent down, scooped me into his arms, and headed toward the stairs.

The brave part of me—the fighter—wanted to hit him and claw at his eyes. If I was going to be killed, I needed to have evidence of his DNA all over me so he would hopefully get caught. But something prevented me from doing so. Maybe it was the fear, or the exhaustion, or the insane mind fuck I had just encountered. Whatever it was, I remained motionless and allowed this man, this kidnapper—this killer—to carry me up the stairs and out of my dark prison.

8

P ope sat me down on a simple wooden chair
with a floral cushion next to a large wooden
farm table in the kitchen. The sun beamed through
the lace curtains that hung over the large windows
that were on two of the four walls. I had no idea
what time of the day, or even what day it was,
which added to my disorientation. The kitchen
reminded me of something plucked right out of a
Home and Garden magazine. Martha Stewart herself
could have decorated it for all I knew. It had a
country charm with the bright yellow walls, the
off-white cabinets accentuated with antique brass
handles, and the oversized farm sink sunk in
against large slabs of dark granite that made up all
the surfaces. The refrigerator was far larger than
they would ever need for two people, but it

matched the masterful aura of the room. China plates of different patterns hung on the walls adding to the charm. If I wasn't kidnapped sitting barefoot in my captor's cotton shirt that smelled of his masculinity, and scared shitless, I would have actually enjoyed having a cup of coffee in a room such as this one.

I pulled my knees up to my chest again, feeling the strong urge to cover every inch of my skin with the oversized shirt. My survival skills were kicking in as I scanned the room for a way out of my hell. There was a door that led outside, but the large windows in the room showed me that we were indeed in the woods. All I could see were thick stands of trees all around. So even if I somehow made it out of the door and ran to the woods to hide—then what? I believed Vivian when she said we were out in the middle of nowhere. I was barefoot. How long would I survive against the elements of the woods with no idea which way to even run? I also noticed a knife block nestled up next to the toaster on the counter. There were six knives tucked into their proper slots.

Pope pulled me from my thoughts of planning my escape when he said, "I don't know where to begin."

His mother stood behind him, and by the intensity of her trembles, and her worried face, I could only assume she was still Viv. Pope leaned up against the counter and studied me as I sat in a ball on the chair.

Viv took a few steps toward me, but stopped when I flinched at her movement. "I'm sorry. So sorry."

I looked at her, then at Pope, and then back at her. "Why am I here? What are you planning to do to me?"

I wanted to cry, but I didn't have any more tears to shed. I also didn't want Pope to know how truly broken I felt. If he knew how weak and frightened I was inside, it would give him more of the upper hand. But my head swam, my heart pounded, and my gut wrenched. I wasn't sure if I was going to be tortured, get raped, or even die in this sick and twisted game they were playing. I don't know why I expected a kidnapping to be more black and white than this. It was as if I was expecting something that wasn't playing out as I had thought. I had absolutely no idea how this story was going to end. In fact, I had no idea what the next line in the paragraph was going to be. If Pope and Vivian had planned to fuck up my mind, they had definitely succeeded in their mission. It was like how a cat toyed with its prey before finally killing it. A cat never mercifully executed the mouse or bird. No, the cat continually gave the victim hope by allowing it to move, to feel free for a few moments only to be pounced upon again, all before eventually meeting its demise. Pope and Vivian were the evil cat toying with me, but that also meant my demise was near.

"Nothing," Pope said with firmness and even anger lacing the word. "Nothing at all." He still had no shirt on, which only added to the bizarre element in the room. "My mother is," he looked at her and then at me with sadness in his eyes, "sick."

"I know," I said softly, but that still didn't explain why they kidnapped me. And why was I even talking to them? I should just lunge for the knives and stab one in their throats before they saw it coming. Just like the movies, I could suddenly have super human powers and the thirst to kill with a vengeance.

"Not just the Parkinson's. She is sick in other ways." I could see that Pope was struggling with what he wanted to tell me. Though he was still powerful in stature and appearance, his face and eyes told a different story. "She has split personalities. There is another person who comes out in her. One that she can't control." He looked at Viv who was staring down at the ground, appearing ashamed by her son's confession. "The other personality inside her did this."

Was this all part of the cat toying with the prey?

"I don't need to know why you kidnapped me. I just want you to let me go." I looked at Pope and then Viv frantically. "I won't say a word. I won't tell anyone. Please, just let me go, and I will never say a word. Just don't hurt me."

Viv looked up from the wood-planked floor. "My son had no part in this. He didn't know." I wasn't sure if I rolled my eyes, or if my obvious disbelief was evident on my face, because she added, "She kept it all secret from him. She made sure he didn't know. It's why she had me keep you quiet the entire time. It's why she had me drug you."

"She?"

"Vivian. Vivian did this."

Pope slammed his fist onto the counter causing both Viv and myself to jump. "How the fuck did this happen? How did she get here? You couldn't have done this yourself. How?" His voice mastered the room and sent a chill down my spine. When his mother didn't answer but only started to cry instead, he looked at me and asked, "How did you get here? Who did this?"

Could it be? Could Pope truly have had no idea his mother kidnapped me?

"You had no part in this?" I asked with narrowed eyes.

"None."

"I find that hard to believe. How in the world could you have no idea you had a drugged, tied, and gagged woman in a box? How the fuck could you not know you had a naked and kidnapped woman in your wine cellar?" Anger sizzled my core. "Who the fuck do you take me for? There is no fucking way you weren't part of this, so don't even try lying to me! Just let me go! I just want you to fucking let me go!" I stood up, my legs feeling weak, and for a second I worried I would collapse right there. "You drugged me, you packaged me in a box, you loaded me on a truck, and transported me here by plane all to be your captured bride! Don't you dare stand there and act like you have no idea what is going on! I don't know why you and your mother are playing these games with me. Why are you doing this?" Tears cascaded from my eyes and my vision blurred. "Why? Why?"

Pope grabbed his mother by the arm. "Who helped you do this? There's no way you could have done this by yourself. Who helped you? Tell me!"

Viv appeared terrified by her son's aggressive behavior. "Richard," she squeaked.

"Who the fuck is Richard... Your handyman? The man who helped move our stuff?" Pope's voice intensified in volume. "The man knew she was in one of those damn boxes of yours? Are you telling me that you both drugged this woman and brought her here? Why the fuck would you do that? What the fuck is wrong with you?"

For a minute, I wondered if he was going to hurt his own mother. The rage coursing through him was obvious in the way the veins in his body pulsated against his flesh. The color in his face reddened, and his jaw tensed with every single syllable of his words.

"I... I don't know what to do. What are we going to do?" Viv looked so fragile as Pope towered over her.

"What are *we* going to do? What are *we* going to do? I have cleaned up your messes my entire life! We're here in the middle of nowhere because of you. My life is destroyed because of you. I have given you everything! I gave you my freedom! I went to jail because of you! So how dare you ask me what *we* are going to do? You fucked me! Do you know what's going to happen to me? When she goes to the police, they are going to lock me up for good. There is no *we*, Momma. There is only *me* and my fucked up life because of you!" Pope slammed his fist against the granite again and then stormed out the kitchen door before I could even take my next breath. The door slammed so hard that one of the china plates on the wall fell and shattered on the floor.

Stunned by Pope's outrage, I stumbled back and sat down on the chair where he had first placed me. I looked at Viv with the odd desire to give her comfort. Something about her still pulled at my heartstrings even though I knew it was because of her that I was in this situation to begin with.

That was, until she looked at me.

Vivian had returned. I didn't even need to hear the southern accent to know she had. I could see it in her eyes. I could feel the energy change.

With a swipe of her hand to wipe away the tears that Viv had shed, she calmly spoke in her elegant and eerie way. "Now, child. Look what you have done. You got Pope all upset." She paused as I watched a surge of strength reenter her body. "He does have quite the temper. His father always did as well. But don't you worry. I know how to handle a fiery passion such as his. As part of your training, we are going to have to work on how to keep a man from losing his temper. It's the job of a good wife to understand how to placate and diffuse the alpha nature of such a man as Pope." She walked over to where the shattered plate had fallen, knelt down, and picked up the pieces as if it were an every day occurrence.

I frantically looked over at the knife block, prepared to grab a weapon. This was the time. Pope was outside, Vivian was on her hands and knees with her back turned to me. This was the moment. Act now!

"It really would be a shame for Richard to have to hurt your dear friend Maria. He knows if he doesn't hear from me at certain times of the day, to start going down my list of things to do to her and that darling baby. The list really is ghastly, but necessary, child. It serves a purpose for a greater good."

I froze, no longer considering reaching for the knife. How could I? What if Vivian was telling the truth and had the ability to really hurt my friend?

"I feel simply dreadful over the fact that I missed

my first check in with him ten minutes ago. With all the commotion and all, I was unable to call him."

"Vivian! Please! Call him now!" Alarm bells rang, fear stabbing at my very core. "Please don't hurt them. They haven't done anything wrong. Please. Please."

"Well, the first item on my list was to slash all four tires. Too bad really. I suppose it's going to take that girl a full week's salary to replace those. Poor Maria. I can only assume that working as a waitress and raising a baby makes her finances extra tight. Though it could be worse. The next item on my list is a fire I believe. An accident of course." She chuckled lightly, looked over her shoulder at me, and gave a wicked smile. "A fire in an apartment building as old as theirs... Can you imagine the risk? I wonder if there are even proper fire alarms installed to warn them in the middle of the night."

"Please don't. I'll do anything you want. Just call him so he won't do anymore harm to them. Please."

Vivian stood up and walked to the trashcan to dispose of the fragmented china. "Anything?"

"Yes, anything. Just tell me what to do."

"I already told you what I wanted. Be a good girl

and allow me to teach you all the ways to be a good wife for my son."

"Okay," I blurted, desperate to say whatever she wanted to hear. "Just don't hurt Maria and Luis, and I will do whatever you want me to do."

She smiled and walked toward the refrigerator. "I thought you would eventually see it my way, child." She pulled out a package of raw chicken and placed it on the counter. "I think what this family needs right now is a good old-fashioned supper. Fried chicken is just what we all need. Comfort food." She glanced over at me before she opened up a cupboard and pulled out a clear container of flour and some seasoning shakers. "Don't worry. I'll teach you this recipe that has been passed down from generation to generation. Food is one way to capture a man's heart for sure. But right now, you need to go outside and make it right with Pope."

I stood up and looked toward the door he had slammed only moments ago. "Make it right?"

"Yes, child. He's simply furious over this entire scene of yours you caused. So, you need to be a good girl and march yourself into his workshop and beg for forgiveness." When I didn't move right away, she added, "His shop is sort of his haven. All men need a haven of some kind I suppose. Pope has always been good with his hands. He likes to do carpentry and builds furniture and such. Just like Jesus, you know. Jesus was a carpenter." She looked at me with annoyance on her face. "Go on now. The workshop's right outside that door yonder. Go make it right and bring him back for supper. If you do that, then Maria and Luis will be all nice and safe for tonight. I'll make sure Richard keeps a special eye on them to ensure it."

I robotically made my way toward the door, but then paused and asked, "Vivian?"

"Yes, child?" She was hunched over, pulling out a frying pan from beneath the oven.

"Did Pope know you were going to bring me here?"

"No. He wouldn't have understood. That boy can be stubborn just like his father. But I know what's best for him. A momma always knows what's best. And in time, he will thank me for all my hard work in making this happen. You will too, child. A momma always knows what's best."

"How could he not have known?"

"Oh, child," she said with a giggle, "men are so easy to trick. You simply have to learn how. But don't you worry. I will teach you the ways just as my momma taught me and her momma taught her. By the time you walk down the aisle with Pope, you will have him wrapped around your finger while he has no idea that you do." She shooed me with her hands. "Now go on. Go pay the piper, though that will be far different than what should happen. Back in my day, an outburst such as yours would have warranted a good old-fashioned whoopin'. But most men these days don't spank their wives anymore for misbehavior. They are weak. A mighty shame if you ask me. Nothing like a strong man who knows how to take his woman in hand." She turned and focused her attention on the chicken. "Go on and apologize and fetch Pope for supper."

9

I padded barefoot across the dried leaves, the pebbles, and the scattered pine needles spread on the yard separating the house from the workshop. I wasn't used to walking around without shoes, so every single step hurt as something or another poked the delicate flesh on the soles of my feet. Pope's shirt went down to the middle of my thighs and covered me sufficiently, but I had never felt so exposed as a cool breeze ran along my bare legs. I had no shoes, no bra, no panties, and no idea what I was going to say to the man inside the workshop.

Opening the large wooden door slowly, I peeked inside the shadowed room cautiously. "Pope? Can I come in?"

His back was to me, and I could see he was aggressively sanding a large piece of wood. He was now wearing a flannel shirt, which he must have had in the shop. Over and over, his muscles flexed as he attacked the wood with every ounce of pent up energy he had. "It's going to be dark soon. I can fly you out of here now, but I would rather not fly these mountains tonight. The wind currents get tricky. It's safer if we wait until morning, but I also understand if you want to leave immediately." There was little emotion in his voice.

I walked into the workshop fully and shut the door behind me, closing myself in with a man I had thought was my captor only to find out that he was clueless. I had no idea what to say to him or where to even begin.

"I also understand if you want to call the police. I don't blame you." He sighed loudly and stopped sanding. His shoulders drooped as he looked down at his worktable. "I moved her here so this wouldn't happen again. I was doing everything I could so she wouldn't be able to hurt another person. But I was too fucking late." He spun around and stared at me as he leaned up against his workbench. "You don't know me, and I have no right to ask you to not report this, but my mother can't control Vivian.

She really is a good person when she's Viv, but simply too weak to fight off Vivian. The woman who truly is my mother doesn't deserve to go to prison. In her condition, I worry it will kill her."

I remained motionless and silent, taking in the man and trying to make some sense of what was going on.

"I also understand that you may not believe me. It seems impossible that I had no idea how you got here. Fuck!" He ran his hand through his hair. "I had no fucking idea, and it kills me that I didn't. I knew she had the potential to do something awful again. I knew it, which is why I made this all happen. This house so far away from everyone so she couldn't hurt anyone." He looked at my bare feet and slowly ran his gaze from my feet to my eyes. "Are you okay? Did she hurt you?"

I shook my head. "She didn't hurt me."

"You must be terrified."

I nodded.

"Demi, right?"

I nodded.

"I'm so sorry. I know that doesn't fix this fucked up

situation, but I want you to know that I am so sorry."

"Why did she do this?" I asked softly.

Pope tilted his head back and looked at the ceiling as he released a deep breath. "I don't know." He looked back at me. "When I was thirteen, my mother suffered from what my father and I had assumed was depression. Then she was diagnosed as bi-polar, and then ultimately we were told she was a schizophrenic. My father tried everything. Medications, clinics, specialists, and even had her committed from time to time. But he couldn't lock away the woman he loved so much. The mother I knew, and the wife he loved, was not this Vivian who showed herself. And there were years that Vivian rarely was around. There was even a little girl personality who called herself Vivi." He paused and looked as if someone had just punched him in the gut. "Vivi hasn't been around for years. I think Vivian got rid of her, and I fear it's just a matter of time until Vivian gets rid of my mother completely. My mother has no control of her. And no matter how hard I tried to fix her, there was no fixing. I spent my entire adult life trying to make her healthy. I spared no expense. And every time, I failed. And just when I would get ready to give up on her and simply have her committed forever, the momma I loved would return. I would see the loving woman I cared so much for smile at me. I couldn't do it to her. I couldn't hurt my momma. There's a good side to her. A person who would never have kidnapped you. I know this must be impossible for you to believe."

"I've met that woman. I met Viv at the diner. I had to help feed her because of her condition."

He nodded. "She told me of a waitress who helped her. She really liked you and was grateful for all your help. Her Parkinson's is getting worse, and it appears that Vivian is getting stronger. Her medical issues don't stop there. She also has congestive heart failure and has been having mini strokes. She doesn't have a lot of time left, and Vivian seems to be overpowering her far more often than she ever used to do before." He looked back at my bare feet. "Let's go inside, and see if we can find some shoes that will fit you, and some clothes before we leave."

"We can't leave," I blurted.

"You'd rather wait until morning?"

"No. We can't leave at all. We can't." My heart sped up as I made the declaration. Hearing the words leave my lips, made my terrible situation all the more real.

"What are you talking about?"

I took a deep and shaky breath. "Your mother." I swallowed against the large lump in the back of my throat. "Your mother told me that if I don't do what she asks, she'll hurt my friend Maria and her new baby."

Pope shook his head. "I won't allow that to happen. There's no way she can leave this house without my help. The only way in and out is by plane. It's too far for anyone to walk, let alone her."

"Richard. She gave Richard a list. A list of things to do that will hurt Maria." Tears welled up in my eyes, but I blinked them back. "He's working for your mother, and if she doesn't contact him at certain times, then Maria will pay the price. I can't allow that to happen."

Fresh fury exploded from Pope as he stormed toward me. "I won't allow it! I'll stop this insanity right now! Enough is enough!"

I reached out my hand and stopped him by pressing it against his chest. "No! Please no!"

He froze in place. I wasn't sure if it was the panic in my voice, or that he knew deep down he couldn't stop his mother.

"I can't risk it. The thought that your mother could hurt Maria and her baby makes me sick. But I can't risk Vivian getting angry and somehow following through on her threat."

My hand was still on his chest, and he slowly placed his own hand over mine. "Let me fix this. I'll go talk to my mother right now and have her call Richard off." The warmth of his hand on mine was the first piece of comfort I had had since this nightmare all began, and it did seem to help soothe the absolute terror threatening to engulf me. Something about his soft touch released the floodgates, and I began to cry. "They are all I have. Please don't risk it."

"I can help."

"Can you? Can you really? Do you think that your mother is capable of hurting someone like she claims?" I sniffed back my tears as the tiniest bit of hope entered my heart.

He removed his hand and walked back toward his workbench. "She's capable of it."

The haunted tone of his voice sent a shiver down my spine, and fresh tears fell again.

"She's hurt someone before. She's killed before."

"Who?" I don't know why I asked, or if I even really wanted to know the answer.

"My past girlfriend. My mother killed her by running her over with a white SUV all because my momma deemed her as not worthy of her son." He spun around and looked at me again. "But it wasn't my momma who did it. It was Vivian. I know that might not make sense to you, and you may think I'm just as crazy as you think she is, but that woman who kidnapped you is not my momma. My momma is the sweetest, kindest woman who would never hurt anyone willingly. She's just very sick and very weak."

"So what do we do?"

Pope remained silent as he stared off at nothing in particular, lost in thought.

"I have to stay," I answered for him, wiping away the tears as renewed strength came to me. "At least for now. I can't have Maria and Luis getting hurt. I have to do whatever I can do to save them. And if that means playing along with your mother for now, then that is what I have to do."

"No," he said as he shook his head. "It's not safe. You being here, taken the way you were, has proven to me that my mother is far sicker than I even thought. We have to get you out of here. Get you safe."

"No. I can't risk it. Your mother already had Richard slash Maria's tires as some kind of warning to me."

Pope sighed loudly and looked up at the ceiling again as if searching for an answer that simply didn't exist.

"At least for now. Your mother is expecting us to walk back into that kitchen and eat her fried chicken as if nothing has happened. If I don't return with you, and if we don't sit down and eat like a perfect little family, your mother is going to teach me another lesson and have Richard do whatever is second on her list. So, for now, we have to play along. We have no choice."

Saying the words out loud gave me a sense of power I hadn't felt since the moment I closed my eyes on my little blue couch. Yes, I was the victim and at the mercy of a crazy woman, but I had some control. I could control whether Maria and Luis were harmed. I had *some* control no matter how little it was.

"Demi—"

"It's not ideal. It's the most fucked idea I have ever

heard or had in my entire life. But it's our only choice. It's *my* only choice. If you go in there and demand for her to stop, you are only going to anger Vivian. You said yourself that your mother was too weak to fight Vivian off. So right now, you can't reason with her. You can't force her to stop her plan. All we can do is placate her until we figure out a way out of this. All I know is I don't want Maria to pay the price for us not going inside and eating chicken. If I have to fake it and do whatever Vivian asks me to do to save my friend's life, then I will. Please tell me you will too. Please."

"It's not safe."

"No, it's not."

"This is insane. Playing her game is insane."

I looked down at my appearance and put out my hands for emphasis. With a smirk, I said, "I think everything about this situation is insane. I think that's fair to say." I grew serious again. "But I don't see another option right now. You yourself said she is capable of hurting Maria and her baby."

"Yes, she is. But she can hurt you too while you're here. If you upset her—"

"I don't think she'll hurt me."

"She will. She's done it before. I never thought she was capable, but Vivian is dark and evil. She can. I thought I could keep my girlfriend safe, and I was proven how wrong I was, and it cost an innocent woman her life. If you do one thing to upset her—"

"Then I'll work hard at not upsetting her. We both will need to. She doesn't want to kill me. She only wants to turn me into the perfect wife for you."

"Fuck! Which is fucking insane!"

"But we have no choice. We have to do this for right now. I really do believe deep down that, as long as I play along, she won't hurt me or Maria."

Pope remained quiet for several moments, scrutinizing every inch of me as he contemplated my plan. Finally, he said, "The minute I feel your life is in danger, the minute I feel she no longer wants you as her forced daughter-in-law, I'm pulling the plug. I'll have you on that plane and out of here immediately. Maria and Luis or not. And this isn't permanent. Only until we figure out how we can stop her and Richard."

I nodded in agreement.

"And you need to listen to me. I know her. I know my mother, and I know Vivian. You don't act on your own. I need to know that we are on the same team."

I nodded in agreement again.

He placed his hands on his knees and bent at the waist as if he needed to catch his breath. "I can't believe this is fucking happening." There was so much pain in his voice. Remaining hunched over, he lifted his head to look at me. "I don't know how, but I will fix this."

"We need to go eat chicken. One step at a time. Right now, that is our plan. Let's go eat supper and play along. We need to make sure she believes you and I are both okay with her plan."

Silently, he walked toward me and picked me up into his arms, cradling me close to his chest. His eyes still held the pain he felt, but they also held something new. I could see a strength, a determination that had replaced the shock that had filled him from the moment he saw me in the cellar. He seemed to grow somehow... as if becoming even stronger... protective if that made any sense at all. Silently he walked. This man had gone from being my captor whom I feared, to my coconspirator in this sick and twisted plan. "We need to get you shoes." His words came out in small puffs of air that caressed my cheek only inches from his mouth.

I didn't say another word as he carried me across the yard and entered the house. Vivian was waiting. Dinner was waiting. The fucked up game of being Vivian's puppet was waiting.

10

"Just in time," Vivian said in her thick southern accent. She noticed Pope carrying me into the house and beamed with pride. "Such a gentleman my son is. Makes a momma proud to see her son turned out to be such a proper young man. Demi, you are a lucky girl. A lucky girl indeed."

I noticed Pope's jaw clenched as he lowered me to the ground. He was extra careful to make sure that his shirt continued to cover all my private areas. Up until this moment, I had only seen Viv around Pope, but right now Vivian was the one cooking this supper and greeting us with that syrupy voice of hers.

"Go ahead and wash up," she said casually as she

put a bowl of peas on the table that was already set for three.

Pope silently walked toward the kitchen sink and pointed toward an archway leading toward a hallway. "Feel free to use the bathroom."

I did as he asked, in desperate need of using it. When I returned, both Pope and Vivian were sitting at the kitchen table. If someone were spying on the scene from the window, it would appear as a normal family dinner. That is until I walked in still barefoot and wearing Pope's shirt.

I sat down at the table and tried not to look Vivian in the eyes. I was scared... terrified that any minute she would snap on me.

"Isn't this nice," she began. She reached out her hands to each of us to take hold. "Let us give Grace."

I took her tiny fingers in mine, then took Pope's much larger hand that engulfed my own, and stared down at my plate of fried chicken, peas and mashed potatoes. Pope's palm was warm, and he gave me a slight reassuring squeeze. I needed it. My courage wavered, and I wasn't sure I was going to be able to keep up this charade.

"Dear Lord, we give thanks for the food before us,"

she started. "Your bountiful gifts to us are appreciated. Please watch over my son and his soon-to-be-wife. Help them in their budding courtship and help guide them to live a Godly and pure life. Give them the strength to act according to your plan. Amen." She looked up at me as I mumbled 'amen' as well and locked eyes with me long enough so I could see a warning in them.

"Amen," Pope said. Without looking at either his mother or me, he picked up his chicken and began eating. I could see he was struggling with the illusion that all was fine, and I wasn't a captive held against my will pretending to be a part of a happy little family. It was obvious he knew how fucked up this situation was, wasn't in denial over how crazy and dangerous the woman who'd kidnapped me was, but was determined to keep me safe, and that little bit of knowledge helped me feel less out of control. I had someone in this with me. Pope was on my side, and knowing that little secret gave me the strength to keep going.

"After supper," Vivian said as she too picked up her chicken and nodded at me to dig in, which I obediently did, "you can take a shower and clean up. Your clothing has been unpacked, hung, and folded neatly in your room."

"My clothing?" I asked, surprised she had packed my belongings as she was having a man shove me into a moving crate.

"Consider it a gift, child. I went out and bought you a whole new wardrobe fitting of a soon-to-be-wife. Trousers and some of those masculine items you wear just aren't proper attire. Someone as pretty as you, and with the curves you have, should be accentuating that fact. I bought a bunch of lovely dresses, skirts and blouses, shoes, and even some undergarments that I think will look quite lovely on you. I'm sure Pope will appreciate seeing you dress more feminine." She looked at Pope who still hadn't looked up from his plate. "Isn't that right, Pope?"

He didn't respond.

"Pope? Isn't that right?" she asked again with more force.

He glanced up at me, and I tried to plead with my eyes for him to continue to play along. He had to for the sake of Maria and Luis.

He took a deep breath. "Yes, Momma."

"I might have gone over budget a wee bit."

"That's all right, Momma," he assured her before

quickly shoveling a spoonful of potatoes into his mouth as if to keep himself from saying anything further. From saying what he no doubt wanted to say. What any normal man would truly want to say.

She smiled proudly. "I knew you would agree." She looked at me and leaned in to whisper, "I have a feeling Pope is going to spoil you rotten. His daddy always spoiled me too."

I gave a weak smile and forced the words to come out. "Thank you. I appreciate your kindness."

"Now, Pope is the man of the house, so his word is the final say of course. But I gave you your own room. I'm not so old-fashioned to believe that kids these days need to wait until marriage for sex, but I thought it best to give you your own room so—"

"She'll be sleeping in my room," Pope interrupted.

His abrupt declaration surprised me, and I almost argued that I wouldn't be staying with him, but he shot me a look that had me closing my mouth. I couldn't pinpoint exactly what it was, but I decided to discuss it with him later. We were on the same team, and I had to remind myself of that.

Vivian opened her mouth in surprise, but then quickly regained her composure as she sipped from her water glass. "Like I said, Pope has the final say." She gave me a wink. "Men."

I watched her scoop up a spoonful of peas without even the tiniest of shakes. How was she able to simply turn off the Parkinson's when she wanted to? It made no sense to me at all. The Viv I had come to know would have never been able to eat peas without several constantly falling off the spoon.

"Do you not like the meal?" Vivian asked. "You've barely eaten a thing."

"I'm not hungry is all," I answered as I tried to take another bite of the chicken, hoping I wasn't offending her.

"I completely understand, child. It's been a long day, and I'm sure your travels have plumb tuckered you out. You're excused to get in the shower so you can settle in early tonight. You'll find a nightgown and dressing robe in there waiting for you. I also left a bag of some essentials for you with directions. The bathroom with the good shower is at the end of the hall. Not the one you just used to wash your hands. You'll want that fancy shower head if you know what I mean." She giggled, smiled widely, and then used her manicured hand to shoo me off. "Don't worry about the dishes and cleaning up. I have it all covered. Now go on, child. Take your time."

I put down the chicken and glanced over at Pope who gave me a slight nod to do as Vivian suggested. "Okay, thank you," I said as sweetly as I could muster.

Without waiting for another response, I got up and padded my way to the bathroom at the end of the hall. A shower and clothing that consisted of more than Pope's shirt actually sounded really good. And the alone time beneath the stream of water would help me gather my senses. The chaos of my world muddled my thoughts. I couldn't tell if I was making wise choices or foolish ones. Should I try to call the police while she and Pope were in the kitchen? Maybe they could rescue me in some type of covert operation. Would Maria and Luis get hurt if Vivian got arrested before she could give the command to Richard? But then I remembered her saying that if she didn't check in at certain points, bad things would happen. No, I couldn't risk trying to be the superhero and risk the lives of two people who had no idea they were being used as pawns.

I closed the bathroom door and was pleased to see there was a lock. Turning the tiny lever and hearing the click of the lock engaging was the first time since this awful ordeal I could actually breathe normally. Not that I was safe, or anywhere close to it, but I was alone and locked in a room by myself. Although the momentary sense of security vanished the minute I saw the pile of clothing with a brown paper bag resting on top. I didn't have to lift the material to see that the nightgown Vivian spoke of was nothing more than a sheer pink nightie with delicate lace around the hem. The nightgown wouldn't really conceal an inch of my body. There weren't any panties to go along with the lingerie either. But at least there was a satin robe that would hide the sexy attire, though even the robe would barely cover the cheeks of my ass. There was nothing *ladylike* about this, and it surprised me that Vivian would pick out something so scandalous when she was preaching not long ago about *proper* ways.

I picked up the brown paper bag to see what was inside it. Not sure what to expect, I was relieved to first see a razor, a folded piece of paper, and then a box which I couldn't make out what it was at a quick glance. I grabbed the paper, unfolding it to read what turned out to be a letter, my relief instantly morphing into shock.

Dearest Daughter,

Please enjoy and use these items to enhance your hygiene.

First, I noticed earlier while I was cutting off your awful clothing that your little kitty had far too much hair on it. A proper wife does not have a bush such as the one you have. It is simply unsanitary and quite unsightly. Please use this razor to shave it all off. All of it. Be extra careful around your clit, and be sure to spread your pussy lips to get all those pesky hairs inside. Though it is fair to say that there are several styles one can choose for the grooming of her pussy, in this case, I think it best to be completely bare. That is, until Pope tells you otherwise. So not one little piece of hair should be present when you are done.

Second, is the box inside the bag. It is an anal douche. I would like you to cleanse your anus with it every single time you shower. There are directions on the box if you need, though I think it is pretty clear what you do with it. I will keep a supply under the sink at all times, no worries there, child. A proper wife does not have a dirty bottom hole. You must keep it clean so it is ready if Pope were to want to use it as he sees fit. It is important when you shower, that you are clean in all ways.

I do hope you will not be defiant in my wishes. I will be checking when you are finished with your shower. If

you choose to ignore my wishes, you will be punished...
or should I say, that Maria will be punished for any act
of rebellion. It would be such a shame for Maria to
suffer the consequences of you having a hairy vagina
and a dirty anus. A shame indeed.

Remember... Momma's watching. Momma is always
watching.

~Vivian

CRUMPLING UP THE LETTER INTO A BALL, I THREW IT
at the wall in disgust. What the fuck was wrong
with this woman? This was far more than having a
multiple personality disorder. She was perverse.
Not only was what she was asking me to do
disturbing, the fact that she was asking me to do it
at all made my stomach turn. An anal douche!
Shave my *kitty*! Just as I was about to storm out of
the bathroom and irrationally give the woman a
piece of my mind, there was a knock on the
bathroom door.

"Is everything all right in there," she asked in the
kindest of voices.

I cleared my throat to regain some sort of
composure. "Yes."

"Did you get my letter?"

"Yes."

"Why are you not in the shower yet? You don't want to be in there all night. Chop, chop." There was a pause. "I would hate to miss my check-in with Richard because you took too long in the shower. I can't check in with him until I can be sure you are following my directions."

My ears rang and the walls of the bathroom seemed to be closing in on me. "I'm getting in now."

Almost robotically, I turned on the water, removed Pope's shirt, grabbed the little brown bag, and entered the shower without the slightest care of what the temperature was. I had no choice but to do exactly as Vivian demanded. My pride was not worth Maria's safety. If I had to stick the anal douche up my ass every day to ensure her safety, I would. I would do anything.

Everything about the shower was a blur. I washed, I shaved, I cleansed all areas inside and out, but it all whirled in my head as I struggled to hold onto reality. I had no plan. I had no solution. I had no way out. All I knew was I had to play along for now. I had to. And when I finally stepped out of my shower, with a bare pussy, and a cleansed bottom hole, I dried off while staring at my reflection in the foggy mirror. Who was this woman staring back at me? She appeared so haunted, so lost.

"Demi?" Pope's voice came from the other side of the door. "Is everything all right?"

No! Nothing was all right. "Yes," I called as I reached for my see-through nightie. "I'll be out in a minute."

"Can I get you anything?"

Freedom? "No. Almost done."

I finished dressing and looked down at my bare pussy. Somehow the pink sheer fabric didn't conceal the fact that there was no longer any hair covering my sex. If anything, the gown almost seemed to draw attention to that spot—as if announcing the fact that my pussy was now bare.

"I'm going to go turn out the lights and close up the workshop. I'll be right back, and we can then go to my room and... talk. Is that okay with you?"

I nodded, not that he could see me. "Yes." Maybe then we could come up with a plan. Anything. Anything to wake up from this sick and demented nightmare. Anything.

11

"Oh, now don't you look lovely," Vivian praised as I padded barefoot back into the kitchen. "I knew that nightgown would fit you perfectly. And the color pink accentuates your complexion and coloring splendidly. You look like a little doll. A delicate little doll."

My wet hair dripped down my back, as I hadn't taken the time to dry it. I was far too worried that something else would happen to Maria if I remained locked away in that bathroom any longer.

"Let me show you something," Vivian said as she walked over to me with her phone in hand. "Richard sent me these." I looked at a picture on her phone of Maria standing by her car with the slashed tires. Vivian then showed another picture of Maria squatting down and examining a tire. I knew my friend well enough to see the anguish all over her face caused by the vandalism.

I bit my lip so hard to prevent me from saying something I would regret, that I actually tasted blood.

"Hopefully, we don't have to do anything else to Maria tonight. But that's up to you and if you listened to me. Lift up your robe and nightgown so I can inspect you," Vivian ordered harshly.

"I did as you asked." I took a few steps away from her and anxiously glanced toward the kitchen door leading toward the workshop in hopes that Pope would walk in any minute and save me from this bizarre request.

"Lift up your robe and nightgown. I don't have all day. Come now, unless you want Pope to see you bent over the kitchen table with your lady parts in full view. How embarrassing that would be for you."

Clenching my jaw, I followed her disgusting command and lifted the material away from my lower half.

Her eyes scanned the bare surface of my pussy before she said, "Bend over the table."

I took the few steps required to reach the table and placed my belly on the cool wooden surface. I gasped when I felt Vivian touch my pussy and run her fingertip along the freshly shaven skin, and then I gasped even louder when she spread my ass cheeks wide.

"Very good. You got all the hair removed. Even in the tricky spots."

Without warning, Vivian put her finger at my anus and pressed in. The dry invasion stung, but the shock of what she was doing had me crying out in surprise rather than discomfort. I bucked up, only to have her hold me down with her hand between my shoulder blades. Her finger was still rooted in my ass and going deeper with every movement I made.

"Stay still, child. I'm just checking to see if you used the douche properly."

I looked toward the door again, but this time not in hope for Pope to enter and save me. Now, I was terrified he would walk in, see me in this condition, and see what his mother was doing to me. The mortifying thought had me whimpering and wiggling as Vivian gyrated her finger in my tight little hole.

"Stop your whining. It's just a finger. It's nowhere near the size of a man's penis. My goodness, if you carry on like this over a finger, then you better get this little hole prepared by stretching it. A proper wife allows her husband anal sex whenever he chooses. And not with all the carrying on and crying of an anal virgin. So you better get used to something up there mighty fast." She pulled out her finger which had me gasping loudly again. The dryness of her skin against my tender flesh burned. "Looks clean to me," she declared. "You were a good girl and cleaned yourself nice and good. Well done. I knew you would be a quick study in the ways of being a wife. I simply knew it."

Vivian helped me stand up and smoothed out the nightgown and robe with her hands.

"So, you won't hurt Maria now?"

Vivian patted my arm. "Not tonight I won't. Your friend and her baby are going to be nice and safe because you were such a good girl. But that doesn't mean Richard won't have to do something to her tomorrow morning. But that's all up to you, of course. If you follow my direction for what I expect tonight, then Maria and her baby can have a nice breakfast together with no worries."

"What do you want me to do?"

"Well, since Pope has decided you will be sleeping in his room tonight, we have to speed up my plan on training you a bit. I was hoping I wouldn't have to go into this part of the training quite yet, but you kids today. Always so fast and in a hurry." She walked over toward the sink of dishes and began washing them as she spoke. "So, one of the first things you need to learn is that a man loves to have his cock sucked." She glanced over her shoulder at me. "Don't stand there and look so shocked. It's a fact, and the reason I am telling you is that I simply want the best. So tonight, you are going to suck Pope's cock."

"What? No!" When I saw her features harden, I swallowed back my outrage and quickly changed my tone. "I mean, I was going to save all of that for marriage. For our wedding night so it's special." Would tricking this woman work? I doubted it, but I had to say something.

"Oh come now, child. Don't play the virgin act with me. I know you kids these days. And I know my son. He hasn't waited either. I know, I know," she said as she scrubbed a dirty plate with a yellow sponge, "my momma used to tell me the story too. Why would a man buy the cow if he can sample the milk for free? I know. But things have changed. It's not like it used to be. A man these days needs to sample often to give him the confidence that his cow is worth buying. That's why you are going to suck his cock tonight. Give my boy a little sample."

"Vivian, I—"

"Again, it would be such a shame for Maria if you didn't," she interrupted. "And you are all cleaned up and look so pretty right now. You are all set for a seductive blow job. All set, indeed."

Tears burned the back of my eyes. "Please don't do this."

"And before you think about faking that you did and lying to me. I want you to remember that Momma is watching. I'm always watching. Richard is too. He's keeping a close eye on me. It's amazing what you can do now with all those fancy nanny cameras they have to catch a misbehaving babysitter. I couldn't believe how easy it was to hide cameras inside items you would never assume. It's fascinating. When Richard helped me set everything up, I could hardly believe it myself. The video footage all goes straight to my computer and to Richard's for that helpful second set of eyes.

Fascinating." She looked out the window. "Pope's returning. So remember to do a good job. Lick his cock from base to tip, and then tip to base over and over again. Oh, and men like when you take their balls into your mouth. I want to make sure you do that. I'll be paying close attention to the footage tomorrow to see if you did a good job. You better do a good job for Maria's sake."

I stood speechless. I had no idea how to even respond. Her words weren't fully sinking in. It was as if my brain was blocking out the level of lunacy as a way to protect my own sanity.

"But try not to give it to him all tonight. Spread it out. Start with a blow job, then tomorrow we will move on to something else. Give the boy a little tease. Play with his emotions and desires a bit." She turned and gave me a large smile. "Now, a good wife knows how to give a good blow job, dear. So go on inside that room and lick his cock like a dutiful wife would do." The door to the kitchen opened up and she quickly added, "And remember that Momma is watching."

Pope walked in and scowled when he saw me standing in the nightie and tiny robe. His look reminded me of the same expression he'd given when he had seen me sitting naked and tied to a chair.

"Are you ready for bed?" he asked between gritted teeth. "It's been a long day."

"Oh she's more than ready," Vivian answered for me. "You kids get a good night's rest. We have so much to do tomorrow to get everything unpacked and set up just right to be our perfect family home."

Pope didn't say anything as he walked up to me and gently took me by the upper arm and led me out of the kitchen. "Are you okay?" he whispered when we reached the hallway.

I didn't answer. I couldn't bring the words to form in my mouth. How was I going to do this? How would I survive this sick game if I was expected to have such vile and filthy acts done to me like having a finger shoved up my ass by an unhinged woman? Vivian expected me to suck on the penis of a man whom I didn't know. She expected me to do it all while cameras were recording me. How was I to survive this? I couldn't! There was no fucking way!

"What was my mother saying in there? You look

white as a ghost. Did she do something to your friend?"

I shook my head and whispered, "Not yet."

"Good," he said as he guided me down another hallway to where there was a large doorway at the end of it. "Then we will keep doing whatever we have to do to placate my mother. Whatever it takes."

Yes... whatever it takes. I knew I needed to do whatever it took or Maria and Luis would suffer. I knew Vivian wasn't bluffing. She had already proven to me how serious she was by showing me the pictures of Maria inspecting her ruined tires. I knew Vivian wouldn't simply kill her and the baby because that would give away all her power, but she could definitely make their lives miserable for each misbehaving act of mine. So, yes, I would have to do whatever it took, even if that meant giving a blow job to Pope against my will.

As we entered Pope's bedroom, I released a breath I hadn't realized I had been holding. Maybe it was the door closing and the sound of the lock he clicked, or maybe it was the warm shades of burgundy and wine colors that made up the room, but something about standing there beside him made me feel an odd sense of comfort. The walls were made from polished logs, and the ceiling was arched with massive wood beams. A large master bed with an intricately carved headboard sat in the middle of the room. Fluffy pillows with a beautiful quilt all in warm red colors meshed perfectly together. The room smelled like the shirt of Pope's I had been wearing —masculine.

I padded barefoot on the wide, wooden-planked floor to a sliding glass door that opened to a private deck. "It's beautiful. You have your own oasis here."

Pope walked over to a brown leather chair that sat in the corner of the room next to a lamp and tiny table. At the foot of the chair sat a basket full of books and magazines. He began removing his boots as he mumbled, "It seems I'm in need of this *oasis* more now than ever before. We both are."

There were two Adirondack chairs on the deck that I imagined having coffee in on a beautiful morning. If I were here at this house for any other reasons, it would be a true vacation paradise— especially this master bedroom. The large slider and the huge window to the left of the bed looked out onto a picturesque view of the woods. Large pine trees, redwoods, and aspens, reminded me of a fairytale setting.

"There's an attached private bathroom behind that door," he said.

I looked over my shoulder to see him kicking off his last boot. Pope leaned back in the chair and ran his fingers through his hair. I was about to ask him a question when I remembered.

Momma's watching...

I glanced at the corners of the room for any signs of cameras and couldn't tell where they would have been placed. The large rafters made it impossible to see if cameras were hidden among them. We couldn't talk safely in the room. I knew this, but I had to somehow tell Pope. "Can we go outside?"

"Outside? You aren't exactly dressed for the evening temperatures."

I reached for a red-checkered flannel blanket that hung over the edge of the bed and wrapped it around me. "I could really use some fresh air," I said as I walked toward the slider. "Actually, I wish I had my cigarettes. A smoke is highly needed right now."

Pope stood and walked toward a dresser and pulled out the top drawer. "Smoking is a nasty habit, Demi," he lectured. "But lucky for you, I suffer from that same bad habit." He pulled out a package of cigarettes and a lighter before pushing the drawer closed.

I walked outside with Pope right behind me. The brisk air made contact with my face, and had I not had the blanket wrapped tightly around me, I would have been cold for sure. But as I lowered myself into the low-seated chair, I felt cozy and content.

Pope sat down beside me, lit a cigarette, and then passed it to me. He then lit his own cigarette and took a long drag before speaking. "I try to save them for a special occasion. But if having a kidnapped woman in my bedroom isn't a special occasion, I'm not sure what the fuck is."

I couldn't help but smile. I wasn't sure if it was his sick sense of humor, or simply knowing I was going to inhale the sweet taste of nicotine any minute. "Yeah, I think we both get a free pass right now."

Remembering the question I had wanted to ask, I did so now. "Why did you insist I sleep in your room rather than my own?"

"Do you really need to ask that?"

"Yes. Why?"

"Because my mother—Vivian—is dangerous. No

way am I going to trust her in the middle of the night. Who knows what she's capable of doing to you? I had no idea she was capable of kidnapping you. That's for fucking sure. So no way am I going to give her the opportunity to hurt you." He took another drag before adding. "You'll be safer in here with me behind a locked door."

"Makes sense." And it did. As long as I didn't upset Vivian, I was sure I would be safe. But with her temperament and her crazy demands, who knew how long she would remain happy with me?

"I'm sorry."

"I know," I said on exhale as the smoke left my lips. "I don't blame you."

"You should."

"Why?"

"I should have stopped this long ago. I shouldn't have been stupid enough to think I could manage my mother on my own. I knew she was dangerous. I should have had her locked away."

"She's your mother. Trust me, I understand all about having a fucked up mother/child relationship."

"I still should have prevented this. And I sure as

fuck shouldn't have been so blind as to not know that she had a kidnapped girl in our moving van and the back of my goddamned plane."

I smirked and took another relaxing drag. "Yeah, I'm still not sure how she managed to pull that off."

Pope turned his head and studied me for several seconds before saying, "I'm sure people are looking for you by now. No doubt the authorities are involved and it's just a matter of time until they track you down."

I shrugged. "Maybe. But I doubt it. I don't have any family, and frankly, I have a history of picking up and leaving without even saying a goodbye. My only friend was Maria. I had a shitty waitress job, an even shittier apartment, and not much worth returning back for to be honest." I smirked again. "Your mother must have done her homework. There's no one to miss or worry about me. I'm the perfect candidate for someone to kidnap and not draw any attention to the situation." I looked at him with a raised eyebrow. "Fucked right?"

Pope looked straight ahead at the forest that served as our view. "Yeah, fucked."

12

———

I wasn't sure how long Pope and I sat out on that porch smoking our cigarettes in silence, but knowing what I still had to do, I could have remained there all night. I sat with my legs tucked up against my chest, and the warm blanket cocooning me inside the soft fabric. The wooden deck felt like a lifeboat I didn't want to disembark. I closed my eyes, savoring my false sense of security.

"You're tired," Pope said, the first in breaking the soothing silence. "You can have the bed, and I'll make a pallet on the floor."

I shook my head, knowing now was the dreaded time to tell him what needed to happen. "No. We have to sleep together. Your mother will know if we don't."

"No, she won't. What happens behind that door is our damn business. She can believe we are, or whatever the fuck she wants."

Taking a deep breath and trying not to cry, I took in his powerful body, his face, and then his eyes. I didn't want to cry. I needed to remain strong and composed. I wasn't going to give Vivian the power of any more tears. "She has cameras, Pope."

Anger sizzled in his deep brown eyes. "No fucking way."

"Yes, she told me. She said Richard helped her set them up. She said they are everywhere, and she'll be watching the videos. She also said that Richard has access to the footage, and if he sees us do anything to harm Vivian or act out in any way, that his instructions are to go down the list that Vivian made for him of ways to hurt Maria and Luis."

Pope didn't say anything. He took a deep breath and stood from the chair.

"Even if we found the cameras, we can't risk turning them off or breaking them. I believe your mother when she says she'll do something bad to my friend. I believe her."

"I believe her too."

He paced in front of me from one side of the deck to the other. "So, let's discuss a plan."

"The only plan for now is that we have to sleep in the same bed. We have to give off the image she wants. We have to do every single thing she asks of us. She wants us to *court* as she puts it."

"Fine. Fine. Fuck!" He stopped pacing. "We'll sleep in the same fucking bed if that'll make her happy."

I flinched at his fury. Though understanding it, Pope's loud, booming voice startled me.

"There's more," I said softly.

"More? What?"

"I've been given a task to do tonight, or else."

"What task?"

I swallowed, breaking the stare that Pope and I had. How was I going to say this? Heat ran along the surface of my cheeks, and my mouth grew dry. "I have to... I have to—"

"What? Tell me!"

"I have to give you a blow job," I blurted as I stared at the splintering wood to avoid seeing Pope's reaction.

"What? Are you fucking *kidding* me?"

"She said I have to. For the sake of Maria."

"No way! This has gone far enough. This is fucking sick. I'm not going to allow this any longer. Enough is enough!"

"Shh," I said as I brought my finger to my lips. "If you keep yelling like that, she's going to hear you. Stop and be quiet. Please!"

He opened his mouth, but then closed it as he took a deep and calming breath. He looked up at the sky as he did so.

"It wasn't a suggestion of hers. It was a demand. And one I plan on doing to keep my friend safe."

Looking back down at me in disbelief, his eyes wider than I had ever seen them, he asked, "You're serious?"

"We have to, Pope. Vivian threatened starting a fire while they slept. God knows what else is on her evil list for Richard. But I can't risk it."

"So what? We go inside and you suck me off while my mother watches? This is the sickest shit I've ever heard!"

I nodded. "It *is* fucking sick, but something I'm willing to do."

"I can't believe this," he mumbled to himself.

I stood up, still gripping the blanket tightly around me. "We need to go inside so I can get this over with. So *we* can get this over with."

Without waiting for a response, I walked back into the bedroom. I could hear that Pope was walking in behind me, no doubt feeling the same sense of dread that I was. The sound of the sliding door being closed heightened my awareness that my little sanctuary on the deck was blocked out by a heavy pane of glass.

Closing my eyes for a quick moment and taking in a large breath of air, I mustered every last ounce of strength I had. Walking over to where Pope stood, I dropped my blanket and stood on tiptoe to place my lips by his ear. "Go sit down in that chair. Pretend you like it. Don't give Vivian any reason to retaliate or punish me for telling you her plan."

Thankfully, Pope didn't argue. I didn't have the strength to deal with any resistance. I was already balancing on a tightrope of fear. The slightest shove would have sent me tumbling into the abyss of absolute horror.

Silently sitting, Pope looked at me with compassionate eyes. I could feel him. I could hear his silent words. They were reassuring. I'm not sure how, but I could sense his supportive words. I could feel them. And whether he knew it or not, Pope gave me the added power to take the next step.

Untying the belt of the tiny robe that covered my see-through nightie, I anxiously locked eyes with Pope as I lowered the satin to the floor, exposing me completely with nothing but pink sheer fabric on my skin. Pope's eyes remained linked with mine. He surprisingly didn't look at my breasts and hardened nipples. He didn't glance down to discover the sheer fabric did nothing to conceal my bare pussy freshly shaven for him. He didn't gawk at my nakedness but rather remained focused on my eyes alone. He gave me that dignity. He gave me that privacy even as I took small steps toward where he sat, prepared to take his dick into my mouth. Maybe Vivian was watching that very moment, or maybe she wouldn't watch until the next morning. But regardless, I was going to push that awful thought and visual to the deepest recesses of my mind. I would not give her the power of disgusting me any further. It was just

Pope and me now. I was only going to focus on Pope. Nothing more.

Kneeling between his legs in front of the chair where he sat, I looked up at him with pleading eyes. I silently begged for him to offer no fight. To allow this. Allow me to do whatever it took to protect my friend. I wordlessly begged that he allow me to take control.

As if he could read my thoughts, he gave me a slight nod of permission. He reached out and caressed my cheek in a loving act of reassurance. It was as if he had to offer some light on this dark situation. He was compelled to offer the slightest bit of affection even if it was only a soft touch to my face.

I reached with shaky hands for the button on his pants and undid it with the ease of a woman who had done this before. I was like a dying fish out of water, but I would pretend to be a mighty shark. If I pretended to be strong, then maybe, just maybe, I would be able to hold onto a little bit of that strength to allow me to survive this situation. When the button unfastened, and after I lowered the zipper, Pope reached for my hand to stop me. His eyes told me he was having second thoughts.

Survival was on the line.

No time for second thoughts.

"Pull your cock out of your pants and put it in my mouth," I ordered in a stern whisper. I wasn't asking. I was demanding just as Vivian was. "Now."

"No," he said as he went to zip up his pants.

"Please. Pope."

He froze, scrutinized my face and then did as I asked. He removed his cock with his hand, but didn't let go. It was as if he was shielding himself from my assault. And it was an assault. I was going to rape his dick with the touch of my lips and the lick of my tongue, just as he was going to rape my mouth. A sexual act against both our wills.

Seeing that he was beginning to waver again as his body tensed, I placed my fingertips on his hand that still held his cock. The simple touch made his penis twitch, and I could see it start to harden. Feeling encouraged by his slight sign of arousal, I gently pushed away his hand and captured Pope's hardening dick into my palm. It grew as his breath hitched. He didn't want this, but his body did. I could see, I could *feel* that it did. I glanced up at him and watched as Pope closed his eyes and leaned his head back into the leather of the chair. Pleasure replaced every other emotion that was once on his face as I eased my hand down his shaft and then back up again. Looking back down at his dick, I saw Pope Montgomery at full sexual arousal, and what an impressive sight it was. I had never taken a penis of that size into my mouth before. It was thick and tall as it stood ready for my tongue to lick along its extraordinary length.

Feeling my pulse speed up, and my own desire throb between my legs, I parted my lips and brought them to the tip of his cock. The minute they made contact with his sensitive flesh, Pope moaned. This was happening. We both knew at that very moment I was going to fuck Pope with my mouth.

Rising up on my knees so I could help ease the motion of lowering my mouth onto him fully, I sank his cock all the way to the back of my throat. He was rooted completely into my mouth. I circled my tongue around the mass that spread my lips wide. Up and down, I began this forced blow job. Tightening my lips around his cock, I bobbed my head as his moans pervaded my ears. I was pleasing him... and I liked it. I liked it so much that I pressed my mouth all the way down, deep throating his member until I gagged and tears slid from my eyes. Enjoying the only power I had—the power to please Pope—I slowly rose to the tip of his penis, circled it with my tongue, and then lowered him into my mouth, pressing hard against the back of my throat. I wanted all of him. And as he grabbed a fistful of my hair and helped guide me up and down in the rhythm he desired, I obediently followed his direction. Up and down, I sucked. Up and down, I licked. Up and down, I felt the slight sting against my scalp as Pope set the tempo.

Everything about the act was wrong. My mind screamed no. My heart ached as my will was stolen from me. It was so wrong, but the hungry need throbbing between my legs disagreed. It was wrong, but it was so fucking right. I sucked, I feasted, I enjoyed every minute as Pope clearly did as well. It was wrong, but my sexual need overpowered all sense. I wanted more. I should have wanted this to be over with, but I only wanted more. The erotic nature of this act only fueled my screaming libido inside. His cock... I wanted his cock in more ways than just in my mouth. I was ravenous and my appetite only grew as his hard dick mastered my wet lips.

Pope's moans grew louder, and I knew he was close to completion. Would I allow it? Have him come in my mouth and swallow? Would I pull out and let him come all over this little pink nightie? Or would

I straddle his lap and have him come deep inside my pussy instead?

Yes, I wanted that. I wanted to fuck Pope. I wanted his cock inside of me.

Just as I was about to pull his dick out of my mouth and sit on his lap, I heard a knock.

A knock on the door...

Another knock.

I froze, his dick still in my mouth as I looked up at Pope who had opened his eyes and looked at the door, stunned by the interruption.

Another knock.

"Pope? Can you help me?" It was Vivian... No, it was Viv. There was no southern accent. "Pope?"

Confused, I removed his cock from my mouth, pulled away, and sat back on my heels as Pope tucked his penis back into his underwear and fastened his pants. He stood—his hard member tenting his slacks—and walked toward the door just as there was another knock.

Still sitting on the floor, struggling to catch my breath, I watched Pope crack the door and look into the hallway.

I heard Viv's gentle voice. "I'm sorry to bother you, but I can't open my medication bottle. She's allowing me to take the medicine tonight. It's been so long since she has, that I thought I should take advantage of it."

"Momma?" Pope remained frozen in place, but then as if seeing for himself that it was his momma and not the crazy Vivian, he took the pill bottle and opened it for her.

"Thank you, son. I'm sorry to bother you."

Pope didn't say another word, but closed the door and locked it once again. He turned and leaned against the wood as if he needed the door to hold him up. I still hadn't moved from my dutiful position on the floor. His eyes locked with mine, and I could still see the desire in their depths. He wanted me. I could see it.

I wanted him. I could also *feel* it.

Striding over to where I sat, he reached down and lifted me from the floor. Embracing my scantily-clad frame tightly against his chest, he did nothing more than hold me. He held me.

Wrapping my arms around his thick torso, clinging to the warmth I so desperately craved, I whispered against his chest, "Please don't ever let me go." I needed him. I needed his touch. I needed his comfort. I needed him so that I could feel safe.

"I won't. I won't ever let you go."

Whatever those words meant, and whatever I wanted them to mean, all I cared about was at that very moment, I felt safe. I felt protected. I needed to be held. I needed to hear his heartbeat against my cheek. God I so fucking needed it.

I just had his cock in my mouth, and I had just considered fucking the shit out of him, but at that very moment, I wanted nothing more than to remain firmly in his arms.

"Let's get some sleep," Pope finally said as he gently rubbed my back.

I wasn't sure why we weren't discussing what just happened before we were interrupted by Viv, but I no longer had the energy to discuss it or try to make sense of a situation of such epic madness.

Silently, I allowed him to guide me to the bed that we would be sharing. We would sleep side by side as a normal couple would do. It was official... Pope and I were courting.

13

The morning sunlight woke me from my dreamless slumber. Ironic how *living* a nightmare prevented me from having them in my sleep. It was as if my body gave me mercy in the sleeping hours to help me cope with my hell of being awake.

"Did you sleep well?" Pope asked. He was propped up on his elbow, staring at me as my eyes fluttered open. How long had he been watching me sleep?

"Yes," I said with a yawn. I stretched my body, oddly feeling comfortable with the fact that Pope's body was mere inches away from mine. His body heat emanated from beneath the covers we shared. "What time is it?"

"It's early. My mother should still be asleep if that's what you're worried about."

"I'm worried about many things, but whether or not your mother is asleep is not one of them," I mumbled as I reached my arms above my head and stretched again.

Pope leaned in and put his lips to my ear and whispered, "I found two cameras in the rafters." He caressed my face as he said the words to make it appear that we were sharing a soft and seductive moment. "So be careful. We have to make her feel as if you are doing your job in seducing me and our courting is going along perfectly. I think the only place that's safe for us to talk is on the deck." He kissed me on the cheek then slipped from beneath the covers and got out of bed.

I watched him as I tried to ignore the delicate tingles that ran along my flesh when he touched me and even more when he kissed my cheek. He was only wearing a pair of shorts and his bare back beckoned my gaze. The muscles, the caramel tone of his flesh, the delicious place where his shoulder blades connected with his spine. He was hot as hell. I was about to fake the most fucked up and dark courtship with the most attractive man I have ever had the pleasure of experiencing.

"Coffee?" he asked as he walked toward the bedroom door.

"Yes. Please."

He glanced at me over his shoulder and used his eyes to signal for me to meet him out on the deck. "It's a beautiful morning today. Let's sit outside and watch for the deer. They like to come and feed near the deck. If we're lucky, we'll see them."

Again, if I weren't a captive, this entire experience would easily be the best getaway of my life. And if you didn't count the crazy loon in the house, the company was not bad as well. Not only was Pope the most fucking handsome man I may have ever encountered, but he seemed kind, considerate, and respectful. Other than his mother, and maybe his temper, I really hadn't seen a flaw yet.

Shit! Was this Stockholm Syndrome? I remembered watching a movie once on the Lifetime Channel where the lead actress fell in love with her captor. I loved the movie, but I'd always felt it was so unrealistic. Who would ever fall in love with the person who kidnapped them? But Pope wasn't the one who kidnapped me, so... so?

When Pope closed the door behind him, I got out of bed, grabbed my robe that was still lying on the floor where I'd left it, and walked on cold wood to the bathroom. I washed my face and then stared up at my reflection in the mirror. I didn't look nearly as haunted as that last time I stared into a mirror. I actually appeared refreshed, bright-eyed, relaxed. Again... as if I were on a romantic vacation.

What. The. Fuck?

Trying to not overthink before I had a cup of coffee kick starting my brain, I finished using the restroom and entered the bedroom the exact same time that Pope did. He smiled at me warmly as he carried in a tray with two mugs, a French press, and a plate of grapes and peeled oranges. If his mother were watching, she would be really impressed with her son's chivalrous act first thing in the morning? Would this make Vivian feel as if I had done a good job in my blow job? I wondered if my sucking off skills had met her approval.

Not saying anything, I reached for the red-checkered blanket, opened the slider to assist Pope whose hands were full, and we both walked outside to where I sat in my comfortable chair again. Pope set the tray down on the tiny side table that separated my chair from his, and also took a seat. His hair was disheveled, and he still had sleepy eyes which gave him a boyish charm.

Pouring the coffee and then handing me a mug, he said, "You know, I've always wanted to sit out on this deck having morning coffee with someone."

I smirked. "Just not with a girl your mother kidnapped to become your dutiful wife?"

He chuckled as he popped a grape into his mouth. "You have a warped sense of humor."

"Yeah, I learned a long time ago, that if you can't find the littlest bit of light in a very dark situation, you'll break. So, now when things are really fucked, I have to find something in it to laugh about. Even if it's the bizarreness of my life." I grabbed an orange and nibbled as I stared into the woods. "I mean, who gets to say that they got kidnapped by a little old Asian lady to become the bride to her son?" I smirked. "That's horror movie material right there."

"*Misery* meets *Bates Motel*."

"Ha. Exactly."

"In all seriousness though, we have got to come up with a plan. *Our* plan. How long are we supposed to keep this up?"

I took a sip of my coffee and raised my eyebrow at him. "Forced blow jobs? Is that what you mean?

How many of those are you going to be forced to endure? Poor, poor you." I giggled, enjoying the sick sense of humor banter.

"I mean... I'm a team player and all. And a man's gotta do what a man's gotta do. So, if I *have* to endure another blow job from time to time, I guess I can make the sacrifice." He gave me a devilish wink.

"But of course. I mean, if you *have* to have a blow job."

"Look," Pope said in a whisper as he pointed to the tree line. "The deer."

I looked over to where he was pointing and saw a doe, a buck, and two smaller deer emerging from the woods. A slight breeze, the sound of birds chirping, and the warm rays of the sun all helped create the most relaxing morning of my life.

"They like to feed on the grass," he said softly. "Every morning I usually see them."

"It's beautiful here."

"It is. It's my haven. I came here this time thinking things would be different."

"With your mother?"

Pope nodded with sadness in his eyes. "I thought if I kept her here, away from anyone she could hurt, that she would be given the dignity to die in a place like this rather than in an institution. I owed that to the woman of my childhood. I owed that to my father as well. He would have wanted her to die here."

"Why do you assume she's going to die? She doesn't give off the vibe that death is knocking on her door if you ask me. Especially when she's Vivian. The woman kidnapped me. Remember? I would say she's stronger than you think."

"That personality is. But my mother is sick. She's on live-saving medicine, and even though she was allowed to take some medicine last night, Vivian has begun preventing my mother from taking what she requires to stay alive. She's getting weaker and weaker."

"That doesn't make any sense to me. How can Viv be getting weaker, but Vivian is not?"

Pope took a long sip of his coffee, keeping his eyes on the deer. "Power of the mind I suppose. It truly is as if two completely different people exist in her. There used to be more—personalities—but, like Vivi, the one I told you about, they all went away. I think Vivian was too strong for them. She killed them all off. Now, I'm afraid that she is killing off my mother."

"Is that possible? Can Vivian get rid of Viv completely?"

"I don't know. Yes. No. Who knows? Multiple personality disorder is so controversial because there is no textbook rule that exists for all. Each person who suffers from this is different. My father and I tried to learn everything we could. But no matter how much we read, and how many specialists we spoke to, nothing matched what my mother had exactly. Her case was original to her. So there is no easy answer."

"When did your father die?"

"When I was twenty-five. His heart gave out. No doubt the stress of my mother helped in that. It was then that she got really bad. Her rock was gone. And he truly was that for her. He nurtured her, cared for her, and really did love her." Pope sighed loudly. "I tried to step into his shoes. My career was taking off, and financially I could offer her the best doctors, a full-time nurse to live with her, a housekeeper, a driver. Everything she could ever need. But I wasn't her husband, so she just got worse and worse. Because of the demands of my career, I didn't have the time to give her the attention she needed. I tried, but it was never enough. There simply weren't enough hours in a day. Not with the type of job I had. I worked long days, every day. Power and money fueled me. It made me feel in control when my personal life was so out of control. I was stupid to think I could just throw money at it."

"Your mother said something about you buying and selling businesses," I said.

"More like I destroyed businesses."

"Oh."

"And while I was busy being ruthless, my mother was getting sicker. So, I hired more staff. I hired more specialists. It wasn't until I started dating Melody that the real nightmare began. My mother seemed happy for me at first. She seemed to like Melody, and Melody was sensitive to my mother and understood her mental illness. But Melody was an attorney and worked about as many hours as I did. My mother hated that fact. She wanted me to marry. And if Melody was going to be that woman, then my mother believed she needed to quit her job. She needed to be the traditional housewife. My mother believed I deserved a submissive woman who cleaned house and did my laundry. One who was waiting with a cocktail and newspaper in hand for when I walked through the door after work, rubbed my feet so I'd be nice and relaxed, and only then served me a delicious dinner she'd spent all afternoon cooking from scratch."

"Yeah, I've heard all about your mother's expectations of a dutiful wife. She said she plans to train me while I'm here."

"Train you? Jesus Christ." He paused for a brief moment. "But yeah, I can believe it. She tried with Melody. Granted, she didn't kidnap her, strip her down, and tie her to a chair, but she did try."

"Was Melody the woman she killed?"

"Yes. My mother didn't think she was good enough for me. I believed she used the term 'too independent' to be a good wife."

"So she ran her over?"

He nodded.

"Why did you get arrested and sent to prison for the murder if it was your mother?"

"I took the fall." He glanced at me, and I must have had a look of disbelief wash all over my face because he added, "I know it doesn't make sense to you, and after those years behind bars, it doesn't make sense to me either. When I got out, I didn't even contact her at first. I paid my dues, kept my nose clean, kept the parole officer happy, and planned on starting a completely different life. Without her." He poured himself a fresh cup of coffee and did the same for me before continuing. "I guess I'm just a goddamn momma's boy, because the minute I got a call from the nurse I paid to care for her telling me she was quitting because Vivian was around far more than Viv, I felt I had no choice but to come back home to her. I came up with the plan to pack everything up and move her here. Out in the middle of nowhere." He pointed at me. "And now this. She clearly had this planned out for a while. Richard, cameras, everything. My fucking life is ruined again because of her."

"Me being here isn't your fault," I said.

"I seriously doubt the authorities are going to find me blameless. And am I really? You are still here. I should have called the police the minute I saw you tied in my cellar. But I didn't."

"I plan to tell the cops you had no knowledge. You're just as much a victim as I am."

We sat there for several minutes in silence, eating fruit and drinking coffee as the deer grazed in front of us. If I pushed out all the madness of how I got to this little piece of paradise, things really were wonderful... for the moment.

"So, how long are we going to keep this up?" he asked, breaking my reverie.

"As long as it takes."

"And if she expects more than a blow job out of you? Are you prepared to go there?"

"If I have to."

"Even if that means having sex with me? What if she wants you to fuck me tonight?" Pope asked, his voice rising.

I took a deep breath, not wanting to confess my thoughts and feelings I had toward him last night, but feeling the only way we were going to survive Vivian was by being one hundred percent honest. "If we weren't interrupted last night, I think we would have had sex."

Pope appeared surprised and then smiled widely. "Wow. You really say it like it is, don't you?"

I shrugged. "I hate lies. I hate half truths. I always have."

"That's refreshing." He sipped on his coffee and

added, "I feel like my entire life has been one fucking lie."

"Me too."

"Really? How so?"

Did I tell Pope the truth? That he wasn't the only one with a fucked up momma and childhood.

"I have mommy issues too," I said with a fake smile. "I'm in that club right along with you. I can add the daddy issues stamp to my membership card as well."

Pope brought his mug of coffee to mine and tapped them together. "Cheers. I guess we have a lot in common."

I gave a tiny, twisted laugh. "Well, that's a good thing since we are about to be married and all." I winked at him.

Chuckling, Pope asked, "Where have you been all my life?"

"Just waiting for the day that you and I could have this fucked up courtship." I extended out my hand in a gesture of a handshake. Pope took my hand in his and smiled as his eyes sparkled in the sunlight. "Nice to meet you, Pope Montgomery. I'm Demi

Wayne. Or shall I say, the soon-to-be Demi Montgomery."

Pope shook his head. "You are sick, woman. Sick."

Enjoying being able to laugh at the absurdity of my situation a bit, I added, "A girl always dreams of being swept off her feet. I just didn't picture being swept off my feet into a moving crate, drugged, bound, and gagged. Sorta adds an entire new and twisted element to the dream, don't you think?"

Pope shook his head and stuck another piece of fruit into his mouth. "So why do you have mommy issues? Did she kidnap your boyfriends for you too?"

"No, you are the only lucky one there. You mother must love you more than mine did me."

"Did? Has she passed?"

I nodded, feeling a knife stab my heart. "Yes. She died the day your mother kidnapped me."

Pope looked at me stunned in mid chew. "What? Really? That is so fucked up. I'm sorry."

"I don't think your mother knew it. I kept my mother a secret from everyone."

"Why?"

I shrugged. "Self-preservation. I don't know." I took a deep breath. "I've never told anyone this. My mother was sentenced to death for killing five people. She used a bomb and was blowing up a building that she deemed wrong and worthy of being destroyed. Five innocent people died because of it. I was eighteen when it happened." I stared at the grazing deer, not wanting to see the shock and pity in Pope's eyes, but still knowing it existed regardless. "Saying the words makes it so real. I've only been thinking them. Never said them. She was put to death the day your mom arrived at my apartment. I was high on sleeping pills and booze, and your mother added to it, and well... lucky me, I get to be your captive bride now."

"Shit."

I smirked. That may have been the best response I could have ever heard.

"Yeah. Shit."

"I didn't think it was possible, but your life may be just as fucked up as mine."

I stood up, sad that I had to leave this little utopia. "I better get ready and go meet Vivian. Who knows what she has in mind for me today? I don't want to risk her hurting Maria because she begins to feel ignored or something."

Pope also stood and gathered the tray. "Yeah, good thinking. We'll come back out here this afternoon for wine and the sunset. My mother will think it's romantic, and you and I can talk further. There's got to be a solution to this fucked up situation."

"Your wish is my command." I walked toward the slider and paused with a smile as I looked up at him and batted my eyelashes in the most exaggerated way possible. "That's what a dutiful wife is supposed to say, right?"

He shook his head with a chuckle. "A warped sense of humor, I tell ya."

14

"It's about time the two of you woke up," Vivian said in the thickest drawl imaginable as Pope and I entered the kitchen. "But I guess after a long night, it's to be expected." She giggled as she returned her attention to wiping down the counters.

Vivian wore a lace-trimmed apron over her floral dress, accentuated with a pearl necklace. She had her classic pantyhose and black heels on. Despite the fact that I was wearing the simple blue dress she'd purchased for me, her proper and elegant attire made me feel underdressed. When I had gone to my room to get ready, the only clothes I could find were dresses or skirts. There wasn't a single pair of pants to be found. I picked the one dress hanging in the closet that seemed casual. Everything else made me feel as if I were about to attend an English tea. Even my undergarments were far too delicate and lacy for my taste. Luckily, she bought me shoes, one pair being simple black flats. I was not a wearer of heels. Long hours on my feet at the diner made the need for heels nonexistent in my life.

"But you do look lovely today, Demi. So very lovely." She stopped scrubbing and glanced at Pope. "Do you both need breakfast? I saw that the coffee had been made and the breakfast tray gone. Breakfast in bed?"

Pope nodded. "Yes. On the deck. We watched the deer." He seemed so mechanical in his speech. It was obvious that he struggled speaking to his mother when she was acting like Vivian.

"How lovely. I so enjoy that family of deer." She looked at me. "I was thinking of teaching you how to make my great-great-great grandmother's famous peach cobbler. Pope loves this dessert, and the family recipe should remain alive for the next generations to come."

I nodded and walked over to where a second apron hung over the back of a kitchen chair. "That sounds good."

Pope studied me for several seconds. "I'm going to go into the shed and finish a project, if that's all right with you? Clear my head a bit."

I nodded and gave him a reassuring smile.

Vivian also piped in. "You go on, son. This is women's work in here. We'll get lunch prepared and call you when it's ready."

Jesus. This was my life. Cooking in a kitchen all day with an insane elderly woman caught in a fucked up version of *Betty Crocker*.

The minute Pope stepped outside, Vivian turned to me. She appeared excited as she clapped her hands together. "Oh, child! You did so good last night. So good indeed. I underestimated your skills. You certainly can suck cock with the best of them. It must be all the pornography these days. When I first had to take a cock in my mouth, I didn't know the first thing to do. I actually thought you had to suck it like you would fluid from a straw. Can you imagine I thought such a thing? I was simply hopeless. It took me a lot of tries until I finally felt I got it right. But not you! You are a natural at giving head, child." She giggled for a moment before adding, "You couldn't see the expression in Pope's eyes, but I could. The video doesn't lie. That boy has it bad for you. I knew he would. I simply knew it!"

The thought of Vivian watching me suck off Pope made me sick. Vomit swirled in my throat, and I worried that I would throw up over the clean kitchen floor.

"It's made me rethink my plan, however. We have to keep Pope hooked. You obviously don't have to seduce him into liking you. He clearly already does. So, now we have to move on to the second level. Love."

"Have you heard from Richard today?" I asked as I tied the apron in the back of me.

"No. Why should I?"

"Is Maria all right?"

"Why wouldn't she be?"

I nodded and gave her a weak smile. I didn't want to upset Vivian by pushing for any more information that she noticeably didn't want to offer to me at this time. "Should we begin on the cobbler?"

"Yes, yes, we will. Plenty of time for all of that. But first, I have to inspect you."

"What?" I asked as I took a few steps backwards.

"Your kitty, child. I have to check your kitty and make sure it is nice and smooth. Your anus as well."

"No," I said as I continued to walk backwards, shaking my head. "No."

Her expression grew firm. "Now, child. No need for hysterics. It's to make sure you don't forget while you are in the training phase of everything. Eventually, cleansing your bottom hole and shaving daily will become second nature, but until then, it's my duty as your future momma-in-law to help ensure it."

The thought of her sticking her finger in my ass again, and rubbing the flesh of my pussy with her frail and wrinkled hand every single day I remained in captivity was enough for me to snap. Maybe it wasn't smart, but I could no longer take another minute of the insanity. "Get the fuck away from me!"

Her eyes widened. "What a foul mouth. A good wife does not speak with such language. Maybe I should soap that mouth of yours to teach you a lesson."

Warning bells went off in my ears knowing she was serious. Dead fucking serious. "You can't do this to me. I've been doing everything you've asked. But this is too much. Too much!" I yelled.

"Did you cleanse?" she asked as she crossed her arms with an eyebrow raised. "Well, did you?"

I hadn't, but I wasn't going to tell her that. "It doesn't matter. This is absurd!" I screamed my words, feeling as if something had been unlocked from deep inside, and my ability to listen to reason was gone. "Stay away from me! You have lost your fucking mind. You need to be locked up."

"That is enough," Vivian snapped. She reached for my arm and took hold. Her unbelievable strength surprised me as she tugged me to the sink. "We are going to wash that filth right out of your mouth! Right out of it!"

"Let go of me!" I tried to break free from her grasp, but her impossible hold remained. "Let go now!"

Thoughts of survival flooded my mind. Should I punch her? Claw at her eyes?

"A good wife knows how to speak like a lady. Curse words are never tolerated. A thorough mouth soaping will do you good."

"Stop!" I said as she stretched her arm to turn the

water on at the sink, pulling me closer. "I'm not going to allow this."

"You don't have a choice, child. A good wife has to be disciplined often until she learns submission. To be a submissive wife takes a lot of practice and a lot of consequence. Submission is not something you are born with. Heavens no. And the youngsters of today require more training than women of my day. The whole feminist belief and all. But don't worry. I will lay down a heavy hand and give you the discipline you need. A dutiful wife is a submissive wife, and you will learn. You will learn indeed."

I struggled to break free from her grasp, only to have her vise-like grip tighten even more.

The kitchen door flew open. "What the hell is going on in here?" boomed Pope as he charged to where Vivian and I struggled, pulling me away from her and into his arms. I clung to his chest, desperate for any sign of sanity. The warmth and familiarity of his embrace gave me a security that saved me from shattering into a million pieces of crazy.

"You better take that girl in hand right now!" Vivian walked over to the knife block, pulled out a butcher knife, and slammed the blade into the nearby cutting board with a force that seemed shocking coming from such a frail hand. "If you let her walk all over you, she'll lose respect for you. A man must be a man!"

"Momma..." Pope walked toward her cautiously, leaving me trembling without the comfort of his arms to protect me any longer. "Let's all take a deep breath."

Vivian tugged the knife free and drove it down into the cutting board again, and then again, and then again. "That girl has the mouth of a sailor. A good wife does not behave or speak in such a way! It's scandalous." She drove the butcher knife into the wood with more force than all the times before. "Inexcusable. A punishment is in order."

"Momma—"

"Don't 'Momma' me." She pulled the knife out of the board and waved it in front of her as she spoke. "There is a time in every marriage when a man has to show his woman who is boss. It may not be easy, but necessary."

"All right, Momma. I'll take care of it." Pope said the words in the calmest voice with his hands up in a peaceful and soothing manner. "You are right. Just put down the knife."

Vivian froze and glanced over at where I still stood, completely stunned. "If you don't punish her, Pope, then I will. Or shall I say, Richard will."

The blood in my veins froze. Maria...

"There's no need to get Richard involved," Pope continued calmly as he took hold of the knife in his mother's hand. "I will take care of it. Don't you worry."

"You'll take that girl in hand?"

He nodded slowly. "Yes, Momma. Whatever you think is best."

I couldn't believe what I was hearing and seeing. But I also saw how Pope was able to diffuse a situation that I had not only believed to be out of control, but a situation that I'd believed would end deadly.

"My daddy used to keep a paddle hanging in our kitchen as a reminder of what would happen if we disobeyed him. And it wasn't simply a warning for us children either. My momma was just as afraid of the sting of that paddle on her backside as the rest of us." She looked over at me. "I bet Demi has never had a paddle hanging in her kitchen before, nor ever feared the sting of one."

I didn't answer, but only stared at her with wide eyes, rendered motionless by shock.

"Which is why she is such a naughty girl. You need to take this woman in hand and teach her a lesson. A lesson she will feel for several days!"

What the hell was Vivian talking about? Did she want Pope to beat me?

Pope placed the knife back into the block and then subtly turned it away so it wasn't as easy for Vivian to impulsively reach for. "All right, why don't you tell me what happened. Why do you feel that Demi should be punished?"

"Her mouth for one. It's atrocious. And she is refusing to follow one of my rules."

"Your rules?" he asked as he glanced at me and then back at Vivian.

"I'm helping her. Guiding her in the ways of a proper wife. I have many years of wisdom to offer. But in order for all my time to not be wasted, it is crucial that she follow every single one of my rules." She crossed her arms and gave an evil smile in my direction. "It would be such a shame for Maria if Demi were to decide to stop following my rules."

My heart stopped at her second threat. She was serious, and now because of my outburst, I may have just endangered Maria and her helpless baby.

"Richard is waiting for my check-in very soon. After what just happened, I may have to give him the bad news."

"No need for that, Momma," Pope said calmly. "I'll handle it."

"How?"

"Don't worry. I'll talk to Demi and make sure it doesn't happen again."

Vivian shook her head. "No, not good enough. Your daddy was always too easy on me, and I was able to walk all over him. I already warned Demi what happens when a rule is broken. I already assured her you were a strong man. But, I know that you didn't have a man in your life teach you how to be a strong and heavy-handed husband. It's necessary, son. So very necessary. So maybe I should show you how to do it effectively this once."

"Show me?"

"Yes. On how to spank your soon-to-be wife."

I was going to be sick. This couldn't be happening. Was this nightmare really transpiring?

"I think I can figure it out," Pope said in a near mumble.

"You'll spank her?" Vivian looked at me and then at Pope skeptically.

He nodded. "Yes. I will take Demi in hand. You are right, Momma. She has to be taught a lesson."

Vivian smiled. "I'm so glad you see it my way." She pointed to the chair. "Fine. You sit there and have her bend over your lap. I think her behavior today warrants a bare bottom spanking."

I felt the blood drain from my face.

Pope nodded, still not looking at me. "I agree. A bare bottom spanking. It's what a man would do." Pope's voice had the mechanical cadence I had begun to realize he used to speak to Vivian when he didn't mean a single word he was saying. I mean... he had to have not believed a single word he was saying.

"Yes. A bare bottom spanking would be enough to make my call to Richard a far more pleasant one, and provide a far better outcome for sweet Maria."

"But not here," Pope said. "I will discipline my fiancée in the privacy of our bedroom. This is an intimate lesson she and I are to share. Not with anyone observing. I'm sure your daddy disciplined your mother in private."

She nodded. "Yes, my daddy always sent my momma to her room to stand in the corner and wait for him."

Pope glanced at me and then at his mother with a nod. "Very well. If it worked for my grandfather, then it'll work for me." He looked at me with an expression on his face so different from the man who'd shared coffee with me only a short time ago. "Demi, please go to our room and find a corner to stand in. I will be in there shortly."

"Pope—"

"Demi," he interrupted. "Did you not hear my mother?"

I could hear the warning in his voice. Everything was so out of control, but I had heard his mother. Vivian had once again threatened Maria if I didn't follow her dictate. I had no choice but to follow her rules or there would be a serious price to pay. Far worse than being spanked like an errant child. I somehow found the ability to make my feet move, and I took the slow steps to Pope's bedroom—our bedroom.

"Wait for one moment," Vivian said as she walked

toward me, her heels clicking on the hardwood floor like tiny bullets meant to kill me.

I froze, terrified at what she would do to me. At least she still didn't have a knife in her hands, but she had just proven to me how strong she really could be.

She walked to where I stood and gave me a hug, whispering in my ear, "After your punishment, you will go straight to the hallway bathroom and cleanse your anus, and shave your kitty like I expected you to do before this all started. And remember... Momma's watching. I am always watching."

A chill ran down my spine as I walked on wobbly knees to the bedroom. I couldn't even look at Pope as shame and humiliation threatened to suffocate me. This wasn't really happening. It couldn't be, and yet it was.

15

Cameras. Cameras. There are cameras. I had to keep chanting the words in my head in order to force myself to do as Pope and his mother had commanded. I knew Vivian would watch the footage of what was about to happen. There was no way she wouldn't. For one, the sick bitch would want to make sure that I paid for my crime properly, and for another, I think she actually would find pleasure in it.

So, I had no choice. I walked to the corner of the room furthest away from the door as if somehow that made me safer, and stood in it with my face inches from the wall. The warm burgundy paint became my only view, and the ridiculousness of the situation actually had me smiling in that uncomfortable and awkward way one couldn't control. Even as a child, I never stood in the corner, though I didn't exactly have a childhood with parents who offered guidance ever. But as an adult... I was stuck in the most fucked up nursery rhyme.

Demi Wayne was a naughty child.

Standing in the corner for being too wild.

About to be spanked on her bare behind.

To teach obedience, Pope would remind.

I struggled to not giggle which then led me to wonder if I had lost my mind just as much as Vivian had. Was I just as fucked and broken as she was? Why did I want to laugh? Why did I have butterflies fluttering in my tummy? With nothing to do but stand with my nose in the corner, I remembered a scene I had watched on *Little House On The Prairie* where Nellie Olsen had been put over her husband's knee and spanked. She was an adult, and her husband had spanked her for being a brat. I remembered that I had been fascinated with the scene. It had given me butterflies then like the ones I had now. Was this really going to happen? Was I about to be spanked like Nellie Olsen had? But that television show was set in the

1800s. Not in modern times. The discipline of a grown woman didn't happen in today's time. Did it? But then again, being kidnapped by a deranged Asian lady to be groomed to be the obedient and perfect wife didn't happen to people either.

The door opened. My other senses were heightened due to the fact that I could only see where the two walls met. I could hear the sound of Pope's boots as he entered the room. What would he do? Was he also chanting *camera, camera, camera*?

I could feel his presence as he came up to where I stood. I could smell his masculinity as his lips moved closer. I could feel the electric bolt sizzle through my core as he kissed me on my neck and then whispered to me so only I would hear.

"This has to happen for the sake of Maria. You know this right?"

I whispered, "Yes." And without having any self control in my body, I leaned into his kiss when I was given another delightful caress right below my ear. I knew Pope was only kissing me like this to hide our conversation, but it didn't take away the fact that his lips against my flesh did something to me. Something powerful.

"We have to maintain the illusion."

"Yes."

"I'm going to tell you sorry now. But it is my one and only time. I'm doing what I have to do, and I need to know that you accept that fact. After this moment, you will let it go. You will not look at me as an abusive asshole. I will not look at you as a victim. We will see this as just another act in order to save a woman and her baby."

"Yes," I said again, desperately wanting another kiss. A trail of kisses leading to more. What the hell was happening to me, and why was my pussy throbbing in hungry need like a horny teenager?

"I'm sorry." He pulled away from our intimate connection, and a second later, I heard a stern and almost terrifying command. "Turn around, Demi. It's time for your punishment."

As if Pope was a puppet master, and he had my strings in his hands, I did as he asked without hesitation. I wanted this over with. I had always been the child who pulled my Band-Aid off in one fast yank.

Pope took me by the hand and led me over to the bed. He sat down on the edge, with his legs spread, and patted his lap. Was this the signal for me to lay over it? His eyes made contact with mine, and that simple and tiny act was all I needed to have the courage to do just that. It was like a dance of submission, but I didn't know the steps. The act of my belly touching his thighs felt awkward. Was I too heavy? I felt too heavy.

No time was wasted as Pope lifted my dress, revealing my bare behind. The ivory g-string panties that I had put on that morning didn't cover an inch of my exposed skin. His finger hooked the top of the lace, and he removed my panties, pulling them down to the middle of my thighs. His effortless skill, without the slightest fumble, told me this man was not a novice in this act. He knew what he was doing. That much was for sure. My bottom half was nearly naked, minus the band of lace panties bunched at my thighs, and the burn on my face grew to an inferno.

"Demi, your behavior in the kitchen this morning is why you are here." He rested his palm on the cheek of my ass and rubbed it in small circles as if preparing me for what was to come. "Do you understand why I am going to have to spank you now?"

I nodded, keeping my eyes closed as if I could

block this humiliation out if I couldn't see anything but blackness.

Without warning, Pope lifted his palm and slapped it down sharply onto my bottom. He spanked me again, before I could process what was fully happening. "When you are being disciplined, I expect you to answer me with 'yes, sir.' " He spanked me again as if to accentuate his command.

"Yes, sir," I replied with a gasp as his hand swatted my bottom harder than the ones before.

"This is punishment. It is going to hurt. It's going to teach you to control your temper, your impulses," he paused to spank me hard two more times, "and putting the lives of others at risk all because you can't act in a way that's so very important you do."

He began to pepper my upturned bottom in a staccato of rapid swats. It stung, and no matter how stoic I thought I would be during this spanking, I couldn't control my movements as I wiggled and writhed to avoid another painful slap to my heated skin.

This wasn't what I expected. I suppose I somehow thought he would fake the spanking, if that were even possible. I didn't entertain the thought that the spanking from Pope would actually hurt. And it did! It hurt!

"Pope..." I had nothing more to say other than his name, but I hoped it would be enough for him to stop the assault, but he only continued on with swat after swat.

I didn't want to cry out. I didn't want to show any discomfort because I didn't want to give Vivian the satisfaction of knowing that, yes, I was truly being punished. She had won. But this spanking was so much more than just an act of pain. As I moved my bare lower half against the denim of Pope's pants, and as his large palm touched such an intimate part of my body, I felt something deeper. Arousal sparked inside of me with each swat of his hand. The pain turned to pleasure, the sting turned to a throbbing deep within my sex. The way Pope held me firmly against him, the way he dominated the situation, and the way he mastered my body caused my pussy to get wet, at the very same time tears filled my eyes. I was vulnerable, and at the mercy of his hand. I hated this, and, yet at the same time, I didn't want it to stop. It was Pope. I wanted Pope. Maybe I was desperate for a touch, for any touch at all, that even something that caused discomfort such as a spanking was still a touch I needed. It was still something. Anything to make me feel. To feel anything but fear, terror, hate, and insanity. With each spank of his hand, I felt a sense of grounding. We were connected. On the same team. As one.

"Are you going to try harder so we don't find ourselves in this situation again?" Pope asked as he spanked my behind in a rhythm that seemed to calm my soul.

"Yes, sir." Odd how right those words seemed. How naturally they fell from my lips.

Pope paused the spanking, caressing my punished skin with his heated palm. "You realize how important it is? How important it is you follow every direction that is given?" I knew he was subtly reminding me that I had to do as his mother asked or risk everything for Maria.

I nodded, focusing on not moaning when Pope's fingertips got dangerously close to my sex. Pope ran his palm from the top of my ass, to where my butt met my thighs.

I relaxed into him, uncomfortable with my vulnerable position, but aroused by his soft touch and silky voice even more. I didn't move, wriggle or fight his caress. I closed my eyes and absorbed every moment.

"It's important you remind yourself why we are doing this. You have to do what is needed."

Pope parted my legs further, opening my crevice completely to his view. What started as a blush, had no doubt reached a level of fiery red against my heated face. Never had I laid across a man's lap, with my ass in the air, legs spread wide, and everything private in full sight. With only a breathless gasp and a slight tensing of my body, I allowed Pope to do as he pleased. Resistance never entered my mind.

His fingertip dipped into the natural contours of my bottom, sliding seductively along my puckered opening. "My mother had one final request before I came in here. You aren't going to like it, but I feel we have no choice but to listen." Pope's finger rubbed over my anus in small measured circles.

My breath caught, trapped in my throat by the erotic desire for him to press past my opening. Anal sex wasn't ever something I had even considered in the past. Many had tried, but that was an off limits area. But something told me that I would enjoy it immensely with Pope.

He removed his hand and reached for something beside him. I kept my eyes shut, clenching my fists in nervous anticipation. Was

I going to be spanked with a paddle like Vivian said had hung in her kitchen as a warning? Was that what she had added as her request?

Moments later, Pope applied something wet and slick to my puckered rosebud that desperately craved to be invaded. He continued to rub and tease by pressing the tip of his fingertip past the tight skin.

I looked over my shoulder, brushing the curls from my eyes so I could see what Pope had in store. In his hand, was a root of some sort, carved into a shape to resemble the tip of a penis.

"What is that?" I asked, never before seeing something like what he had in his hand.

"This is a ginger root that Vivian," he cleared his throat, "carved into the shape that will fit into your bottom." He took a deep breath as if he was uncomfortable with the idea. "She said you would know why your bottom hole is getting punished too." He glanced up at the rafters and whispered, "There's cameras..."

Oh God! Was Vivian doing this because I didn't cleanse my anus as she had wanted? Was she punishing my asshole because of my not doing so?

What the fuck? Was this really happening? Ginger? Carved to look like a small penis?

Pope placed his hand between my shoulder blades and pressed me all the way down again. The only thing I could see was the wooden floorboards below me. I couldn't help but buck against the root as it made contact with my skin. The fear of the unknown and the pressure on my entrance caused all my nerves to spring to life.

He spread my buttocks further apart and pressed the root past the tight hole. I jerked. "Hold still," he ordered.

I whimpered at the sharp bite of the intrusion.

"Relax." He continued to press the root further, demanding access. "I want you to close your eyes and relax."

Relax? Was he insane?

My hands flailed until they found his calves and dug in. My breath hitched with every movement of the root. Inch by inch, the ginger made its passage into my depths. "Oh, God."

The root was almost all the way in, spreading my hole to my limits. My anus continued to stretch, but my pussy pulsated in desire. The tight muscles of my tiny hole gave as I took the thickest part of the root.

I shook my head, my voice strained. "Pope, I can't. It stings."

"Take a deep breath and relax. You can do this." He leaned down and kissed the top of my bottom.

With a final shove that had me crying out, Pope pushed the ginger root all the way to its carved base.

Pope leaned down and placed soft kisses on my lower back, working his way to each cheek of my butt. He moved his hand to my clit and pinched. I pressed against his touch, desperate for the tender reward for my submission.

He continued to rub and stroke my bud, driving my passion to a whole new level. A slow burn began to build in the depths of my canal. A burning that rippled its way through my entire bottom hole.

Pressing down on my back when I tried to struggle, Pope whispered, "It's all right. It's supposed to burn. Focus on my touch."

The burning in my bottom melted any sense of control. I panted against the sensation as the heat grew in intensity. A scorching fire set my insides ablaze.

I couldn't breathe, couldn't move. All I could do was clench my fist, close my eyes and commit myself to Vivian's dictated punishment.

The punishment continued on until I couldn't tell where the fire in my ass started and where it ended. And my pussy... God, I wanted so much more. The burn went so deep inside my ass, but even deeper within my core.

Mercifully, Pope pulled me up gently so we were both standing. He wrapped his arms securely around me, pulling me into his chest. He kissed my forehead as he rubbed light circles over my burning butt. The sting in my ass, and the stinging ginger root, was nothing compared to the throbbing in my pussy. I wanted Pope Montgomery, more than I ever had before.

He pulled away and took a few steps back while taking a deep breath. I felt my breasts growing heavy, starving for his touch as his gaze dropped to my panties still bunched right above my knees. My face heated as my nipples hardened. His stare only made my pussy dampen with need.

"Demi. I hope you know I would give my life for

you. I'm doing what it takes for survival. You get that right?"

I nodded, not sure that I would be able to speak if I tried.

"Go into the hallway bathroom. Vivian said you would know what to do now."

I nodded again, pulling up my panties, but too ashamed to remove the root until I was behind the bathroom door. Without looking at Pope, I exited the room as a million good and bad sensations sizzled through me.

Vivian was standing in the hallway, blocking the bathroom door. Her arms were crossed, and a smug look washed over her delicate and dainty face. "I suppose your tiny bottom hole is on fire right about now. I bet you won't mind flushing it with cool water now. I bet that anal cleansing is something you simply can't wait for." She giggled. "Remember, Momma's watching..."

16

I was lost in my thoughts as I kneaded the bread dough for the evening's supper. I still had found it shocking that this was something I had actually learned how to do. Vivian had been insistent that I knew how to cook from scratch. A good wife knows the way to her husband's heart is through his stomach, was her lecture as I begrudgingly learned how to follow recipes. Since being kidnapped and forced to be trained as Pope's wife, I had cooked, cleaned, learned the ways of proper etiquette, groomed, sewed, massaged Pope's feet, submitting and serving him in every way as Vivian constantly told me an old-fashioned bride would be expected to do. I was so exhausted I could barely see straight at the end of each day.

Thinking of Pope as I manipulated the dough, I wondered what would eventually happen. How long could this all go on? This game had to be wearing on him just as much as it was for me. I had never worked so hard in my life, so by the time sunset fell, I could barely keep my eyes open long enough to undress and collapse into bed. Fantasies were replaced with chores, and sexual need substituted with exhaustion. But that was only allowed *after* I gave Pope his evening's blow job. Every single night, Vivian forced me to suck him off.

Every single night.

Even Pope seemed to grow tired of the forced act.

I paused a moment and brushed a blonde ringlet from my forehead with the back of my flour-encrusted hand. I rolled my shoulders up and down a few times, in an attempt to loosen my aching muscles.

"Vivian is nearly working you to death."

I jumped at the sound of Pope's voice. Turning my head, I saw he'd come into the kitchen. His jeans were dirty, and his sweat stained shirt clung to his chest. His baseball cap rested low on his head just enough to shield the depths of his eyes. Even filthy, he exuded sex appeal. Vivian had had him busy planting rose bushes along the side of the house. She wanted a floral paradise on the property for the wedding to take place. It was all the woman could talk about at meals. How lovely the grounds would be for our nuptials.

"So much to learn to be that dutiful wife of yours." I turned my attention back to my bread making, realizing that my comment had come out entirely snarkier than I had intended. I was just so fucking tired.

Pope walked up to me, placing both of his hands on each side of my shoulders and began to give a gentle massage. "I know how tired you are." He continued to massage as he spoke, causing me to close my eyes and relish the delightful feeling. "I know I haven't told you, but Maria is lucky to have a friend in you. If she knew what you were doing for her and her baby. What you were sacrificing for their safety."

I turned and faced him, my eyes meeting his. I wanted to melt into his body. His touch. His words. Everything.

Pope took a deep breath and a large step backwards. "I want to take you somewhere."

"What? What about supper and Vivian?"

"Vivian went to take a nap. All her bossing you around has worn her out, and I decided to surprise you with a picnic supper. It's the least I can do to thank you for all your hard work and your shocking ability to deal with this bullshit we call our life."

I stood in disbelief. "A surprise?" I couldn't believe he had taken the time to plan it all out. "Now?"

He smirked. "Come on. Let's go."

We walked quite a distance in silence, his arm wrapped around me, and after a while, I began to feel the muscles in my body ease. My breathing calmed, and my heart seemed to beat regularly again. Every time I adjusted my body, Pope would squeeze tighter, enveloping me in his security and safety. I could feel his breath against my neck, feel his body heat against my side. The sense of being protected, guarded and cared for, replaced any thoughts of fear.

"Over there." Pope pointed. "There's a natural hot spring I thought would be perfect to help ease your tired muscles. The Sierras are full of them. You just need to know where to look."

I turned my head so I could look up into his

smoldering brown eyes. "A hot spring? That sounds amazing. I've heard of them, but never have seen or been in one. Are they really hot?"

Pope placed the palm of his hand on my lower back and walked me to the steaming water. "Some are, but this one is the perfect temperature. Go ahead and get in. I'll set up our picnic." With a twinkle in his eye, Pope smiled. "Don't worry, I won't peek."

"Wait. You aren't going to join me?"

"Well, since we don't have suits, I thought I would give you your privacy and let you have it to yourself."

I reached for his hand. "I would like you to come in with me. If you don't mind." I winked and, with a mischievous smile, began to take off my clothes. "It's not like you haven't seen me naked before." I stripped all the way nude, not caring what he saw, and ran towards the water. "Come on!"

"Woman! You really never cease to amaze me." Pope removed his clothes as quickly as he could, following close behind me.

I slowly eased my way into the hot water, almost moaning in delight as the sultry liquid covered my body. I closed my eyes for only a split second, not wanting to miss the full view of the unclothed man before me. I had seen him before, but this time was different. Vivian wasn't watching as well. We were alone. Private.

Being able to take my time and look at him without the madness of video cameras hidden about, Pope's body did not disappoint. Muscled, lean, and mouthwatering, the man took my breath away. He exuded power as he made his way to the water, reminding me of a Greek God.

"Aww, this is exactly what my body needed," he said with a sigh as he lowered himself in.

I tried to conceal my smile. I couldn't help but have images of what my body *really* wanted and needed from Pope.

He looked at me with an eyebrow raised and asked, "What are you over there smiling about?"

I just smiled more and shrugged in response.

He ran his wet hand through his black hair, slicking it back. "I think we're going to have to make a habit of this. Make this our special spot so we can escape crazy town for a little bit." Pope moved his body closer to mine, our legs barely touching. "I know things have been really tough on you. The things that have been asked, the sick game you have to play. I'm sorry. I wish I could fucking fix this."

"I know. But there's no way to fix it. We just have to wait until Vivian is satisfied with my wifely skills, or she—"

"Dies?"

I looked at him, and my heart sunk. "I'm sorry for thinking that."

"It's the truth. The only way this all is going to end is if Parkinson's and all the other health issues finally put my mother out of her misery."

"Do you think Vivian will die too? Didn't you say that Vivian isn't sick?" I rubbed my wet hands across my face as if I could wash away the dark confusion. "I don't understand the split personality thing. I mean... I do. But I also don't at the same time. It's confusing as fuck."

Pope positioned my body so he could move up behind me as he began to massage my neck and shoulders. His fingers were hard but gentle at the same time. The rubbing turned my body to jelly. "I don't have the answers," he said softly. "There was never the perfect answer or an explanation to what was going on in my mother's mind."

"How long do you think we are going to be here?"

Pope stopped massaging, his hands still resting on my shoulders. "That's completely up to you. If you want to leave right now, I'll get the plane ready. I hope you know that. But we also both know that Maria could be in danger if you do. I hate having this hanging over us, but I have no fucking clue how sick and demented this Richard guy truly is."

"He's sick enough to have slashed Maria's tires. I saw proof of that."

"And he helped kidnap you, so I think it's fair to say he's pretty fucked up," Pope added.

"I don't want to leave." I lifted my shoulders up and down, silently hinting for Pope to continue the massage. "Aside from your mother and all her crazy training tasks, this place isn't all too bad. It really is the most beautiful place I've ever been. And my life was pretty shitty back home, so it's not like I'm missing anything. And you are..." I swallowed hard, realizing I was about to open up to him a little too much.

"I'm what?" he asked as he continued to massage my shoulders and upper back.

I shrugged. "I don't know. I guess... well, I wouldn't have been able to get through these last couple of days without you. Your mother has had me do some pretty awful things, that shouldn't be awful normally. I mean, it's different when you are forced to give a blow job or something, rather than wanting to. You know?"

Pope chuckled. "Yeah, I know. It's different for me too."

I looked over my shoulder at him, causing him to stop the massage. "You're so concerned about me, and to be honest, I've been so concerned about me, that I haven't stopped and thought about how this all could be affecting you. There are times I'm essentially raping you. Your mother is making me rape you."

His eyes locked with mine, and I could see sadness within them. "Yes, I guess so. But it's different for me."

"How so? It's still against your will. Even though you have to pretend that it's not. It's still wrong."

"What if I told you that it's not against my will? Would that make me just as much of a monster as my fucking mother? What if I told you that the minute I saw you that first night, kneeling between my legs, I was a goner. You captured my fucking soul. I just... I'm attracted to you in ways than I can't even explain, and as much as our situation is fucked up beyond belief, I can't stop thinking about you."

I looked down at my pruning hands, not being able to handle the intensity in Pope's eyes any longer. "I..." I took a deep breath, preparing for my confession. "It's not all against my will either. I mean, I don't like the fact that your mother is ordering it, or that I know she is watching, but when I'm doing the actual act, it's not all against my will." I positioned my body so that I could look at him straight on. "But then, I think I'm just as messed up in the head as your mother is."

"When I'm around you, sex is damn near the only thing I can think about. I want you, I hunger for you like I've never done with any woman before." His smoldering eyes locked with mine. "I want to respect you," he said softly. "After everything you have been through, I want to give you that. But I also want to just take what I want."

"What you want?"

"I want you. I want to fucking take it. Stop playing the nice guy. I'm sick of playing. I'm sick of games. I'm sick of it all. I just want to do what my body demands."

I smiled as my heart did flips. "Tell me... these demands you speak of." I moved forward so I was inches from his face. "Show me. I'm sick of the fucking games too."

I gasped as Pope's mouth crushed down over mine. I clung to his shoulders, pulling him closer. Opening my mouth to the smooth feel of his tongue, I ached to feel him deep inside me. The feeling was so familiar, but this time the ache would be quenched even if it meant me *taking* what I wanted.

A shudder rippled through me as his hand gently caressed my breast. Pope continued to ravish my mouth as his hands explored every part of my wet and exposed chest. I moaned as a hot surge of hunger rushed through my throbbing pussy. I ran my hands across the hard plane of his muscled torso, all while his fingers continued to stroke my nipples, giving attention to both equally.

Pulling me closer than I thought possible, the hot water splashing between us, Pope groaned, "God, I want you. I fucking need you." Placing hot, wet kisses along my collarbone, he whispered, "I've wanted you since the day I first saw you. There was something unique. You were strong, yet broken at the same time. Something about you that was unexplainable. I think your darkness sparked something deep inside of me."

I clung to him, gasping for air. The heat of the water, the fervor between us, was almost too much intensity for my fragile mind. I still felt as if I was balanced precariously on the tightrope that hung over the deep cesspool of madness. My mind spun, but my body pulsated.

"I'm taking you right here, right now. I can't fight this any longer. I need to make you mine."

I looked into his blazing eyes and nodded. "Yes... yes. I don't want you to stop."

In an instant, I found myself lying beneath Pope on the soft grass surrounding the spring. He kissed his way down my body inch by inch, until his lips made contact with my yearning pussy. I arched my back as he eased my legs further apart. Little by little, Pope began to place soft kisses along the inside of my thigh, gradually making his way to his ultimate target. I tensed as his tongue flicked the sensitive bud that controlled my inner harlot, causing me to moan in pleasure.

A wavering burst of fervency slid into my stomach. Pope continued to suck and lick, pleasuring my very core as he used his roughened fingers to part the folds of my sex, heightening my bliss, bringing me closer to complete ecstasy.

I tensed. Unsure of letting go completely, I tried to fight the wave of passion that my entire being threatened to succumb to. Having him in such an intimate position battled against my insecurities.

Pope continued to circle his tongue along the outer edges of my pussy as if he had a craving that couldn't be quenched. With a thrust of his finger deep within my heat, he whispered, "It's okay. Let go. You're safe with me. Trust me. Let all that darkness go."

His soothing words, mixed with his sensual ministrations brought me over the edge. Light flashed, heat conquered, and hunger satisfied, I could do nothing but release a heavy gasp.

Regaining some control, and with greedy need, I reached out and wrapped my hand around his swollen shaft. Thick and heavy with his arousal, I guided him to my parted legs. Pope grabbed my hips and held me immobile before he thrust his hard cock deep within me. A rush of pleasure ripped through me with a force that took my breath away. Pope groaned as he pulled out almost all the way, just to thrust his hardness back into my tight pussy, as if desperately wanting more.

I gasped at the suddenness of his submersion, even as my body hungered for more. My head fell back as I closed my eyes and reveled in the sensation of lust pulsing through my core. I moaned loudly as my body drove upward to meet his pace, driving his cock even deeper within.

His body felt strong and good so close to mine. I arched my back when Pope slipped a finger to my clit and began to circle, increasing the pressure in my pussy.

"God, Demi. You are the most beautiful, sexual, and passionate woman I've ever experienced," Pope growled as he lowered his mouth to the crevice of my neck and softly nibbled.

His body felt hot against mine, contrasting with the cool breeze against my bare flesh. Another moan escaped my lips as Pope thrust into me hard, again and again, harder and harder, bringing me closer and closer to ecstasy. The building pressure threatened to overflow at any second.

Lifting my legs, Pope wrapped them around his waist. He plunged in and out, going deeper with each pounding motion. Setting up a rhythm, Pope rocked me to an orgasm like nothing I had ever experienced. I cried out his name as heavenly bliss poured through my shattered soul. Pope stared into my eyes as the climax rocked my body, never letting up until he was sure I was fully satisfied. With one more hungry kiss, his muscles tightened, and his breathing became ragged. He moaned deep as he followed me to release.

IT SEEMED LIKE HOURS HAD PASSED AS WE LAID entangled in each other's arm, luxuriating in the late afternoon sun. Pope ran his fingers through my hair, occasionally giving soft and alluring kisses everywhere his hand grazed. I rested my head on his shoulder, rubbing my fingertips along his bare chest. Without another moment's pause, I kissed him, hungry for him once again.

Pope rolled me onto my back with his weight pressed up against me. "If I knew being with you was going to be like this, I would've made you mine a long time ago," he murmured against the kiss.

"I need you. I want you." I kissed him again, hard and demanding.

I wanted him in every way. Having sex with Pope only sealed the deal. I didn't ever want this moment to end.

I love you, Pope. The words stayed trapped in my

throat, locked tightly in my mind. So close to declaring my feelings, but afraid of the true power those words could release. I wasn't afraid of telling them to Pope, but rather what would happen if my demons heard me say them. Demi Wayne was not allowed to love. The devil in my soul dictated that as so. A broken girl cannot love. A shattered soul is incapable. I knew this. I absolutely knew this.

Pope paused, studied me for a few long moments, then shifted his weight on his side. "Where did you just go? Something changed just now."

I shrugged. "Nothing really." No way would I confess that I'd been about to proclaim my love, but then realized I was entirely too messed up to do so. "I'm just taking this all in, I guess."

He tucked me close, caressing my stomach. "There's a lot to take in lately. The kidnapping, the craziness of my mother, the threats against your friend and her baby, the fact that Vivian actually believes we will be married, and then you and me."

I snuggled closer, playing lightly with his chest hair. "You and me?"

"I'm not the man for you. My life is so fucked up, that there is no way I can pull you into my hell."

"My life was already hell even before I met you."

"Not like this, and you know it."

I sighed. "My mother always used to sing this nursery rhyme.

Jack and Jill went up the hill to fetch a pail of water.

Jack fell down and broke his crown,

And Jill came tumbling after.

She used to tell me to find my Jack. That when I find the man I am meant to spend the rest of my life with, I will be willing to tumble down with him." I closed my eyes, trying to block the sound of my mother's voice as it was too painful to remember. "She's right. And with you, I'm prepared to climb that hill and tumble down with you. Broken crown and all."

"Even if my darkness swallows you up?" he asked.

With a nod and smile, I managed to roll Pope onto his back so I could trace a hungry trail down his body. I kissed, I licked, I tasted my way down to his hardened shaft. I moved my way lower and lower until the tip of my tongue touched the tip of his cock.

With his hips rising to meet my seduction, he moaned, "Put your mouth around me."

I followed his command—not Vivian's—and took his hardness deep within. I wanted this. I wanted to do this with no cameras, no orders, no one watching to see if I sucked him off like a dutiful wife would do. I wanted to do this for Pope. For us.

By doing so, I was able to reclaim the control that I'd had stolen from me. I was doing this by my free will. I had the power—not Vivian.

Swirling my tongue in small circles, I relaxed the back of my throat to allow his size to be engulfed completely. His gasp, his shudder and the way his hands grabbed at my hair, only drove my need to please even higher. I worked my lips up the base, then drove them back down in a rhythmic motion. I drove myself to meet his demands. Tightening my lips, and licking lightly, I worked his cock, intensifying his pleasure. Slowly up, then plunging back down, I worked until his control snapped. His breath hitched and his moan reverberated through his entire body as he climaxed in my mouth.

The moment ebbed, satisfaction blanketing us both. Pope pulled me in close as I wrapped my arms around him and clung tight. I was his. I would always be his.

17

We both stood on the porch, staring into each other's eyes. I didn't want the day to end or reality to slip back in. The last few hours had been a dream from which I didn't want to awaken.

I leaned forward and kissed his cheek. "Thank you for today. It was beyond anything I could have imagined."

Pope stared for several long moments before running his finger along the edge of my jaw. "I need to tell you that, for the first time, I truly feel I can say the words that seemed an impossibility to say to anyone. I –"

The front door suddenly opened and Vivian was standing there, beaming from ear to ear. "How was your date? You both are simply glowing. Glowing indeed."

"Fine," Pope snapped.

Vivian looked at me and gave an evil smile that I had grown to understand meant she had something in store for me. "I have a letter for you, child," she said as she handed me a folded piece of stationary. "To read when you are alone, of course."

"Of course," I mumbled, feeling as if all the wind had been taken out of my sail.

"Demi and I are turning in early. It's been a long day for us," Pope said harshly.

He positioned his hand on my lower back and led me into the house. He dropped off the picnic basket but continued to guide me past the kitchen, into the room we had been sharing, and straight to the deck. I appreciated how Pope had moved me from one safe bubble to the next. I didn't say anything, but took my seat with a smile on my face. I was happy. I was really happy. Was that sick? Had I lost my fucking mind? Maybe. But I was happy.

"Pope?" I heard the muffled question coming from

inside the room. "May I come out there?" It was Viv. I knew it was her even with the lack of southern accent. Viv had a kindness laced within her words.

Pope opened the slider for her as she walked out to join us. Her body quivered a little, but not nearly as badly as I had seen it in the past. I got up to stand, but she put out her hand, signaling for me to remain where I was.

"I would like to speak with the two of you."

Both Pope and I remained silent. She looked out onto the open field, taking in the view and smiled.

"It's so lovely here. It really is a haven."

"Is there something you need, Momma?" Pope asked. I could see he was annoyed to have her in our special, safe place, but at the same time, I saw concern on his face.

She nodded and then looked at me with tears in her eyes. "I'm so sorry, Demi. I wish I could stop her. I do. I try so hard to fight her back. Sometimes I can win, but it doesn't last long. You don't deserve this. Any of this." Her lower lip quivered, and I noticed her right hand was contorted a bit as it also shook.

"I know, Viv. I know you wouldn't do this if you could help it." I looked at Pope who was scrutinizing Viv's every move. I wondered if he was looking for signs of Vivian returning.

She looked at the chair that Pope normally sat in. "May I sit down?"

Pope nodded and gently took her by the arm and assisted her into the low-slung chair. She smiled again, and stared out onto the field.

"I want to die here," she said softly. "Ashes blending with the earth." She then looked up at Pope. "Which is why I'm here talking with you both." She took a deep breath. "I'm getting weaker. Sicker. I feel it, and my weakness is allowing Vivian more and more control over me every single day. I worry that eventually all that will be left will be the pure evil of her inside of me. And her demented self will not stop until sweet, innocent Demi does exactly as she's told. No matter how wicked it may be. I don't want that. I can't have that. I can't stand by and keep allowing you both to be forced to do this against your wills. I'm raping you! I'm raping you both of all that is good. Love is supposed to be good, and I am destroying that for you both." She began to cry, and my heart hurt so much. I wanted to hug her. Comfort her. How I could hate Vivian so much, but care so deeply for Viv shocked me. But it was the truth. I cared so much for the woman crying before me. "I want to die now. End it all. I need to be the one making the sacrifice so Demi doesn't have to any longer. It's time I die."

"What?" Pope asked as I could see his temper beginning to rise. His entire body tensed, and his jaw locked. "This conversation needs to end. Now."

Viv shook her head. "No, son. We've talked about this before. You know I'm right."

"No," he stated firmly. "Enough."

She then looked at me and reached her hand out. It shook and reminded me of all the days that I had fed her in the diner. I didn't want to touch her, and yet I did. This was Viv in front of me. It was just the sweet old lady who needed my empathy. I took her hand in mine and held it, ignoring how we both shook together in unison now.

With fresh tears in her eyes, she said, "Demi, I want the best for you. You shouldn't be here against your will. You shouldn't be held prisoner. I know what Vivian does to you... what *I* do to you. It's awful. It's perverse. It's so twisted, and yet I can't stop it."

I squeezed her hand. "I know. But you don't deserve to die because of your illness. It's a sickness."

She nodded. "Yes, an illness that is far worse than terminal. I have pure hate inside of me. A demon that I can't shed. There is only one way out." She looked up at Pope. "Please, son. Help me end this horror. Demi deserves her freedom."

"By killing you?" Pope shouted. "Is that what you are asking? No fucking way!" His booming voice caused both Viv and me to flinch, which he saw and instantly calmed. "Momma, there will be another way. We'll find another way."

"No, son. There is no other way. Like I said, I can hold her back for a short amount of time. Like right now. So, because I can give myself a short window if I try really hard, I have come up with a plan."

"A plan?" I asked softly, seeing that Pope wanted no part of this discussion at all, but I was still curious to hear.

Viv squeezed my hand with hers that I still held within mine. "I can call Richard. I can use Vivian's voice. I've been practicing and have heard it in my head for so many years that I'm sure I can master it. I call Richard and tell him that you are married, and I got my wish. That he can leave Maria and the baby alone." She took a deep breath. "But that will only last for so long. Once Vivian returns—which she will—she would only call Richard back and tell him she changed her mind or something along those lines. And then she would figure out a way to make sure it never happened again. So, the only way to prevent her from doing so is to kill myself right after the call."

"Stop," Pope shouted. "I don't want to hear another word about you killing yourself. Do you hear me?"

"It's the only way," Viv insisted. "It's the only way to save Maria and that baby of hers."

I released her hand and stood, walking over to where Pope remained with crossed arms and narrowed eyes. I placed my hand softly on his shoulder as a way to offer support. "Pope's right, Viv. No more talk of killing. We'll figure a way out of this so no one gets hurt."

Fresh tears fell from her eyes, running down her delicate features. "Please, Demi. I can't live with myself knowing what is happening to you. What is happening to my son. He already paid for my crimes once. I can't keep doing this to him. He deserves happiness just like you. He deserves for this all to end."

I walked to her, knelt at her knees, and placed my hands on them, wanting to give some of my strength over to her. "Listen to me. I can survive this. I have Pope helping me every step of the way. I'm not alone. You raised a good man. He's been there for me."

"But I want you both to be happy. Not held captive by my demons."

I patted her knee and then glanced over my shoulder at Pope. "Your son and I are finding our way through this maze. It's twisty, but we'll figure it out."

Pope walked over, lifted me to standing, and took my hand in his. "I promise you, Momma, that I will watch over Demi. No demon will hurt her." He then helped Viv out of the chair and added, "But I don't want to discuss this any further. It's been a long day, and Demi and I really need some time to rest."

Viv looked down at the ground, clearly upset that her request was not met with better results. "Pope, please think about it."

"There is nothing to think about. You just focus on trying to be present. Fight Vivian with everything you have. Rest. Take care of yourself. And fight. You can beat her." He led his mother through the slider, the room, and out the bedroom door. I saw him bend down and kiss her on the forehead, giving her a hug before closing the door behind him.

He walked back to the deck and stared at me for several moments. We both said nothing, but only stared as Viv's words haunted our souls. Without saying anything, he seized the back of my neck and pulled my lips to his. The warmth mastered my mouth and dissolved away all thought and every sense in my body except for touch. A renewed fire from earlier exploded within me, leaving me panting for air—panting for Pope.

He spanned my waist with his strong hands, his fingertips meeting as he pulled me harder against him. I felt his loss of control as a shudder ripped through him. I gasped for breath, aware of the bulge in his pants screaming for release.

The moan that I'd been trying to hold back, escaped me in a tantalizing rush. Pope's hands tightened at my waist. He reeled me into him, molding me to his solid chest with sensual, gentle hands. Feeling more of the hard length of his sex pressing against my stomach, I craved more. I yearned for more of his touch.

I finally remembered to breathe. Lifting my head to look up at him, I saw nothing more than the shadowed outline of his broad shoulders and frame, backlit from the setting sun.

"I'm sorry if I overstepped," I managed, the words weak and breathless.

"You were perfect. You have more compassion than I have ever seen or experienced from a single human being. She doesn't deserve your tender heart. I don't deserve it." He slid his hands lower, cupping my ass. "I love you, Demi. I fucking love you." His husky words sounded like a warning—a strained voice of reason, echoing amongst a storm of hungry need. Was he warning me of his love? Warning me to not love back?

Reckless. I was reckless.

I wrapped my arms around his neck, seeking his strength and command. "I love you, Pope. I fucking love you too." I had no other response but the truth. Rash maybe, but how else to resist a man so able to shatter my common sense?

I ran my fingertips up the center of his chest and

then across to his upper arms. Desire flooded through me as I touched him. Muscles flexed beneath my fingertips, increasing the heat that swamped my senses.

He held me still, lowering his head, kissing the side of my neck with his parted lips. He seduced me with gentleness. "Tell me to stop," he commanded. "Tell me to not love you. Demand I never think of you in that way. My love is dangerous. Loving me can be deadly. Insist I walk away."

I shook my head, not wanting to fight him or to fight the fiery need in my body. "No." It was the only word I could barely whisper. Speech was conquered by sexual need. Ruled by my out of control lust.

In one quick movement, Pope swooped me up into his arms and carried me inside to the bed. My body melted with his as I danced my tongue in the depths of his mouth.

I needed more. I needed to feel his skin. Hastily, I pulled his shirt up over his head and ran my hands down his chest. Relishing how smooth and sleek his skin felt against my fingertips, each muscle clearly defined. Sexual attraction took on a whole new meaning at that moment.

Pope moaned as he kissed me deeper, lowering me down onto the mattress below. With movements as graceful and gentle as before, Pope removed each item of my clothing, and then his as I watched in hungry need. Having his nude body standing before me only made the fire inside blaze to a full inferno. My body screamed for him, my heart demanded, and my soul ached for him to take me. My mind swirled as he placed soft kisses on flesh that my clothing had concealed. Pleasure escalated with every touch and with every moment I lay beneath his weight.

I trembled, my body shuddering with the thought of what was to come. "Please," I begged.

I cried out in desperation as Pope plunged two thick fingers deep inside my hungry pussy. Raking across my clit with his thumb, he twisted his fingers inside. Pulling my orgasm to the surface, I rocked my body against his hand.

Pope's eyes blazed as he stared down at me. "You're so wet for me. I like knowing you want me as badly as I want you."

I nodded, my vagina clenching around his fingers as they moved in and out. "Yes!" My body was on fire. Aching with arousal, I grabbed his cock and began to stoke. "Fuck me, Pope. I need you. I need you, now."

Spreading my legs wide with his hands, he pressed his hardness in, stretching me with every inch forward.

"I want it hard. Hard!" I demanded as I fought to take him deeper and faster.

He took hold of my hips, taking control over my desperately thrusting body. Sinking all the way to the hilt, Pope moaned with ragged breath. I tossed my hair in abandon and cried out against the agonizing pleasure. I felt my release building, higher and higher with every drive of Pope's hard dick. With hard driving strokes, he demanded, he dominated, he claimed my body as his. Mixing pleasure with the bite of pain caused by his thick cock spreading me wide, my pussy spasmed as the orgasm violently rocked my body. Pope gripped my hips tighter, groaning deeply as I felt his come fill my quaking flesh.

Again, our love was the only way to deal with our darkness. The blackness of our lives forced us to survive. We had only each other. Only each other to survive this.

It wasn't until Pope was asleep and breathing

deeply, that I crawled out of bed later that night and retrieved the letter that Vivian had handed to me earlier. I knew I was going to hate what was written on that paper, but I also knew I had no choice but to read it.

My dearest soon-to-be daughter,

I have watched you with pride the past couple of days. You are proving yourself to be quite the capable and obedient fiancée. You are following my directives perfectly, and other than a little mishap that was handled effectively by my son, you have been a very well-behaved young woman. Well-behaved indeed.

But now, we must plan for the next level of training. You have kept your bottom hole nice and clean as a proper wife will always do. Your kitty is always pristinely shaven. But now we must prepare your tiny hole so that it is able to accept Pope's manhood. A good wife takes her husband's cock in the ass without complaint. A dutiful wife allows her ass to be fucked often.

In order to prepare, I have left three training plugs in the bathroom next to the anal douches. These are to be inserted into your anus. They are different sizes. The first one should be fairly easy for you to insert. This will be used so you can acclimate to the feeling of something inside of you stretching you slightly. I would like for you to start wearing it daily for two hours for one week. After that, I would like you to move on to the second one. This one is much larger, but not quite the size of a man's penis. You will insert this one and wear it for the same length of time as the first. The second plug is going to be quite uncomfortable. Especially at the beginning while you get used to it. Then, you will move on to the third plug.

The third plug is going to hurt, child. But this is a sacrifice that a dutiful wife must make. The plug is larger than a man's cock so that, if you are able to train your anus to take it, then Pope's cock will fit inside you with ease. It is your duty. It is what is required of a good obedient bride with a little bottom hole.

Now, since you have been a virtuous student, and so willing to do as I asked, I won't require you to start your anal training until the beginning of next week. You are welcome to thank me for this later.

Oh and, child, remember to use the lubrication sitting beside the plugs. Nothing is worse than a dry insertion.

And remember... Momma's watching. Momma's always watching.

-Vivian

I CRUMPLED UP THE LETTER AND TOSSED IT IN THE trash can.

Sick bitch.

I hated her.

I fucking hated her.

Gazing out the window, and seeing the first hint of light on the eastern sky, was something I was falling in love with. I followed the lines of the newly whitewashed fence that surrounded the garden Pope and Viv had been working so hard to create. I smiled, knowing that even thought it was Vivian who wanted the rose bushes for the wedding, Pope had taken the time to do this for Viv, his momma, because it was something she had always wanted growing up. His little addition, done out of respect and care for his mother, made me feel more connected to him than I already did. He loved his mother, and I loved seeing that side of him. He was a momma's boy, but in the best way possible. Kind, giving, loving, and so protective.

Softer.

Normal.

And when Viv was Viv, and *Vivian* was locked away in the depths of her mind—even temporarily—I loved the sweet, kind-hearted woman as well. I did. God help me, I did. I wasn't going to think about Vivian's letter I had read last night until next week came. The only way I would survive my sick prison was by taking each day one hour at a time. One minute at a time. And right now, this minute, I was content.

Looking out onto the land where Pope worked so hard to build a home filled me with such gratification. I cherished everything about this place, the silence, the peace and the sense of... home. Yes, it was a dark abyss at times. But when it was just Pope and me sitting out on his deck, or Viv and me chatting about nothing in particular, I was able to trick myself into believing I wasn't a captive, forced to submit to a man by his crazy mother. The normal was so very pleasant, even though the madness was pure agony.

I hummed to myself as I rolled out several piecrusts—a couple for now and the rest to freeze for later. Vivian had lectured me over and over that a dutiful wife plans ahead and is always efficient.

With damp and gentle hands, I placed them in the pie tins, excited to surprise my new fucked up family with my culinary skills. Carefully trimming around the edges with a knife, I nearly sliced my finger when something odd caught the corner of my eye.

Pope's workshop had black smoke billowing out from it. My heart plummeted as I tried to figure out what to do next.

"Fire!" My scream was nearly suffocated with terror. "Pope, wake up! Your shop is on fire!"

I ran to the bedroom to find that he wasn't there, and I could see he wasn't on the deck either.

There was no sign of Pope anywhere. He must have gotten up shortly after I had. Or dear God... what if *he* was in the fire? "Viv! Viv!" What if *she* was too? "Viv!" My voice quaked in panic.

Where were they? *Where were they*!

Quicker than I thought possible for my legs to move, I ran out of the house toward the burning building.

The door to the workshop was closed. I couldn't hear anything coming from inside. No screams for help. Nothing. "Pope! Are you in there?"

I yanked open the door of the workshop with all my strength. The smoke and the fumes hit me with a force that obstructed my vision and made my eyes tear. I coughed and wheezed as I tried to make my way inside. I could see the flames engulfing the furniture that Pope had worked so hard on crafting, the wood, and very soon the entire room. Smoke clouded my eyes and made it close to impossible to breathe, and I wasn't even all the way inside. Should I go in? Common sense screamed no, but the thought of Pope burning alive inside compelled me to charge against any better judgment.

"Pope! Pope, are you in here? Please answer me! Pope! Vivian? Vivian!" *Fuck!* Please don't either one be in here, I prayed.

Each beat of my heart pounded against my chest. Fear almost paralyzed me as I scanned the inferno. I continued deeper inside, trying not to breathe in the toxic air. Each gulp of the smoke threatened to consume my consciousness. My head spun, my chest heaved, and my body grew weak. I wondered if I could go on any further, and if I too would die in this blaze.

The air was getting worse and the wooden beams above me were beginning to burn and break loose.

I knew I didn't have much time left. Taking a deep breath and holding it, I reached the workbench that Pope used on a daily basis. Desperate to make my own escape, I scanned the area one last time. With cinders flying through the air and beams crashing all around me, I could only hope that Pope or Viv were not trapped anywhere inside.

Mistakenly, I turned around again to make sure I hadn't missed anything. The haze had grown so thick that I could no longer tell which way was out. My lungs demanded air that I couldn't give. The realization that I could possibly die by being burned alive besieged me with fear.

I charged forward, hoping I was heading in the right direction when I stumbled on something, tumbling me to the ground. It was Viv! Viv's unconscious body was lying on the wooden floor. I scrambled to her, lifting her head as I shook her frail frame in an attempt to wake her up.

"Viv! Vivian! Wake up! We have to get you out of here. Wake up!" Was she already dead?

I tried to pick her up, but realized quickly there was no way I would be able to do so. Reaching under her lifeless arms, I struggled to drag her out. It was the only way to save her from being consumed by the flames.

"Demi! Where are you?" I could hear Pope's voice amongst the popping and crackling of the blaze. He was in the workshop! Was he hurt?

"Pope! Pope!" The smoke burned the back of my throat as I screamed. "Your mother is with me. She needs help!"

I felt his hands wrap around my body, and in one swift move, he picked me up and started to charge past the embers and the roar of the flames.

"Your mother," I said, pointing to the lifeless body crumpled on the ground, but Pope didn't even pause. He only stormed ahead with full force.

Behind us, a splintering beam came crashing down, causing a chain reaction of others to follow. I couldn't tell for sure through all the smoke and flames, but it appeared that one could have fallen where Viv laid. Pope dove toward the exit, spilling us down to the ground. The red and orange flames were all around as Pope pushed me fully towards the escape, rolling both of us toward safety.

Mere seconds from death, we crawled our way to safety and fresh air. Gasping for breath, choking against the pungent vapors still burning the back of my throat, I allowed the tears to escape my body as I realized I had just escaped my death. I had survived. Pope had survived. Relief washed over me as I felt Pope lift me up and carry me further away from the crumbling barn, but then, just as fast—absolute terror rained down.

"Viv! Your mother! She's in there, Pope. She's in there." I struggled to get out of his arms to help him rescue her from the burning building, but he held me tight.

He shook his head, dark ash all over his face. "No."

"Pope!" I screamed, writhing my body against his hold to no avail. "Viv's still in there! You can't let her die. Help her!

Holding me tight, he repeated, "No."

"She doesn't deserve to die. No matter what! She is still a human being. She is still your mother!"

"She asked to die. My momma asked to die." The sadness in his eyes told me he had given up all hope of saving Viv's life.

Realization kicked in. The conversation on the porch. Oh dear God, this was Pope doing as she had asked of us. He was allowing Viv her wish. Her wish to die so Vivian would no longer exist.

"No!" I screamed, no longer trying to break free

from his grip, but not willing to accept his words. "We can't just let her die in there."

"She asked for this. This was her wish. She begged me, Demi. She pleaded. My momma wanted to be put out of her misery. This was her doing. She started the fire. It was all her."

I shook my head in disbelief and wailed as the burning building collapsed behind me. "No, no, no, no, no..."

I clung to his neck, sobbing as he walked toward the house. He then placed me down gently, and ran to the garden hose. Pulling it from its tightly coiled housing, he turned it on full blast and ran toward the burning structure. The absolute destruction of the workshop by the large pieces of wood smothering itself out helped aid Pope in his extinguishing of the flames. Even if he had changed his mind and wanted to run in and rescue Viv, there was nothing left to run into.

She was dead.

Burned.

Turned to nothing but ash.

I closed my burning, irritated eyes long enough to

try to cope with the new level of madness. Chaos was all around. Death. Destruction.

Sacrifice.

I wheezed, every breath I took burned my lungs. I coughed and swiped at my streaming tears with the back of my hand. I needed to help him. I had to help put out the flames so they wouldn't spread to our home... *our* home.

Running to the kitchen, I filled large pots of water and ran them to the fire, pouring them onto the flames as Pope doused the fire with the garden hose. Repeating the steps over and over until I nearly collapsed from exhaustion, not stopping until the fire was gone. Nothing was left but a pile of charred wood, simmering embers, and gray smoke sifting out in small and curly billows.

Eventually, Pope dropped the hose, took my hand, and led me back toward the house. "Christ! I'm so mad at you!" Taking me into his arms, he placed soft kisses in my soot-covered hair. "I'm furious!" He pulled away and glared into my eyes. "I could have lost you. You could have died! Do you get that? Why the fuck did you run into a burning building? What if I had lost you too?" He placed a soft kiss on my lips, stealing whatever breath I had managed to reclaim.

"I thought you were in there." I paused and looked over to what had now become Viv's grave. "I thought Viv was in there. I wanted to save you both."

He pulled away and started examining my body. "Are you hurt? Do you have any burns?"

I shook my head and attempted to assure him that everything was all right. But my breath came in shallow, rapid gasps. My mind fogged and my vision began to give way to darkness. I faintly heard Pope call out my name.

WHEN MY EYELIDS OPENED, I WAS AWARE THAT TIME had passed. The setting sun shining through the window cast shadows along the walls. I was lying in Pope's soft bed, staring into the comforting, loving brown eyes I had grown to love.

"Hello, sleepyhead," Pope whispered as he leaned down and kissed my forehead. "You nearly scared me half to death."

I tried to talk, but the burn in the back of my throat radiated with pain.

"Don't try to speak right now," Pope ordered.

I struggled upright, my muscles weak and my head still spinning.

Gently, Pope placed his hands on my chest preventing me from sitting up any further. "Just rest right now," he soothed.

"Why? Why?" I started to cry, mourning the death of my captor, my friend, my enemy. I hated her. I loved her. And now my heart broke in two as I cried over her death. "Why?"

"You know why. She asked for this."

"But you said no. You said no!"

"She kept begging me. She pleaded with me. My momma cried and asked for my help. You know she wanted it all to end. She needed me to understand. I had to understand." Tears welled up in Pope's eyes. "My momma was so sick, and the darkness that was Vivian was eating her alive. She begged me to allow her to die. I had to. I had no choice."

I wiped at my tears. "She started the fire?"

He nodded.

"Were you in the workshop when she did?"

He nodded again.

"It was Viv who started the fire?"

A single tear escaped his eye. "I held her as the flames engulfed the room. I held my momma in my arms as the smoke suffocated her enough to cause her to pass out."

"Then you left? Left her there to die?"

He nodded again. "Until I heard you calling out. I couldn't see you, but I could hear you."

"She's gone..." I said the words out loud as if hearing them, saying them, would somehow make it more real. Everything seemed so surreal, as if I was floating in a fog. Like I was caught in an eerie afterworld. A world where Vivian Montgomery had no control over me. A world that I could no longer remember.

"And Richard?"

"My mother did as she said she would. Viv contacted him pretending to be Vivian. She stood in the workshop by my bench with the phone in hand. I watched her as she faked a southern accent and told Richard that it was all over. That Pope and Demi had married, and all was good. His mission was over. She ended it. She ended it all."

"Maria and Luis are safe."

Pope nodded as he sat on the bed and wrapped his arm around my shaking body, allowing me to place my head on his chest. "Right now I want you to get some sleep. Your body is in shock."

"Stay here with me. Please."

He kissed the top of my head. "I'll never leave you."

I smoothed my hand under his shirt, enjoying the feel of his skin against my palm. "Pope, I was really scared. I thought I was going to die. I thought *you* were going to die."

He whispered into my smoke-filled hair, "I'll never let anything happen to you like that again. I will always protect you, and I'll make damn sure you never feel that fear again. You will *never* be the victim again."

I stared up at Pope as he tucked the blankets tighter around my body. His face still dirty from the fire, his eyes shadowed with exhaustion. "Being here in your arms, with the entire nightmare of Vivian over, I've never felt so safe, but I have never felt so sad as well."

I began to cry softly against his warmth. It was over. It was over...

He rested his cheek against the blonde and dirty

curls of my head. "You're safe. I'll never let anything harm you again." He whispered the soothing words as he placed soft kisses along my forehead. "You need to get some sleep. We'll talk more when you wake up."

Shivering, I closed my eyes and allowed myself to relax against the warmth of his body. I was so tired that I could no longer prevent my mind from shifting hazily between reality and the nightmare of the fire. I fought the weight of my eyelids to look up into Pope's worried eyes.

He gazed down at me and whispered, "You're safe. You'll always be safe."

19

Tension released from my bones and the nightmare of the fire seemed to fade away as I luxuriated in the lavender scented water in the antique bath tub I had quickly grown to love. With my eyes closed, I allowed the shoulder deep water to take away the aches and pains.

The wooden floorboards creaked as Pope knelt down behind me. "Let me help you wash your hair."

I swallowed hard. The tenderness from someone who just hours ago had lost his mother in a horrendous fire spun the emotions inside me to chaos. Such power, such strength, and now showing such compassion. Rather than wallowing in his own misery. The sweet aroma from the steaming water helped me relax as his strong hands began to massage my scalp, gently scrubbing away the smoke and grime.

"Just lean back and let me do this. Let me take care of you," he soothed.

Firm and gentle, the same hands that had just saved my life. The same hands that had just comforted me until I cried myself to sleep were now caressing their way to my very soul. I closed my eyes and moaned as he pressed against my temples, while raking his fingernails along my scalp. A waterfall of warm water cascaded over my head, followed by a rag softly dabbing at my closed eyelids.

"You're beautiful, Demi."

I opened my eyes and turned my head so I could stare into Pope's eyes. "I've never had anyone do this to me... I mean... for me."

His lips brushed my hair, and he whispered in my ear, "You deserve to be taken care of." He continued to wash and rinse my hair, making my muscles melt right along with my heart.

I reached up behind me and wrapped my hand

around Pope's neck. "I think there is plenty of room for two, if you want to join me?"

"This is for you. I want you to relax. I already showered and got some rest while you slept." His voice was as calm as I felt, even as a heavy sadness still rested on my heart. I was so sad. So relieved. So happy. So many conflicting emotions.

I missed her.

I was happy to see her get what she deserved.

I mourned her.

I relished a sense of victory.

It was just Pope and me, and that made me happy.

I was so fucked up. So, so fucked up.

"Do you think I'm a monster?" he asked softly. "For allowing her to die?"

I shook my head. "You're not a monster. I could never think that. You're a survivor and nothing more."

"You wouldn't have done it though. Even after all she did to you, you were still trying to save her."

"Yes. I was still trying to save her."

"Why?"

"It was Viv lying on that floor. My friend."

"My mother." Pope took a deep breath. "Which is why I allowed her to follow through with her plan. She wasn't planning on telling me or you after we both said no. I think she thought I would still be asleep. But when I walked in on her pouring gasoline all over my shed, she pleaded with me to understand. She wanted to die and become one with the earth she loved so much. She wanted her sickness to end. She was in so much agony."

"I know," I whispered. "It took so much strength for her to do what she did. For what you did."

"And now we move on. We have no choice but to move on."

I wasn't sure what moving on meant. How do you move on after terror has dominated every inch of your being?

"Viv would have wanted us to move on," I agreed.

His hands made their way to my shoulders and began to work the same magic he had done on my head. Pope's hands continued to stroke, the movements unhurried, lingering, stretching over my collarbone down to the tops of my breasts in slow easy circles.

"Your body..." his voice rasped.

Over and over, he ran his calloused hands along my breasts, barely grazing my nipples with each pass. Tingling and fire grew within my core, my pussy longing for more.

I needed the pain to go away. The confusion had to end. Anything but this. Anything to overpower the darkness.

His momma had just died.

This was wrong.

But nothing about our lives had ever been right.

The need, the hunger, the passion building as the warm water washed over my skin. A bolt of sensation shot through me as Pope caught the sensitive tip of my nipple and gently pinched. My gasp no longer able to be contained.

As if the gasp was Pope's green light, he continued down along my stomach. His fingers sliding their way to my bare sex—as Vivian had dictated it to be so. Without hesitation, he cupped his hand around my mound and slid his finger between my needy lips. Finding my clit, he rubbed softly. Coaxing my pleasure, rather than demanding it.

Pope used his other hand to cup my breast, while he placed searing kisses along my neck. I lifted myself into his touch, spreading my legs wider for his access. I needed more. I needed to feel him deep within me. I needed to be taken, conquered and mastered.

"I need you," he said huskily between the kisses along my flesh. "I need my pain to stop. I can't fucking take the pain."

"Please... Pope... please," I could barely get out. "I need the pain to stop too."

"Just us. I need it to be just us. Leave the fucked up world we live in behind us. Just us. Now." Pope increased his pressure on my clit and rubbed my nipple in between his fingers, keeping a steady rhythm, driving my need to a boiling point.

I couldn't take it any longer. I grabbed his hand and directed his finger to the entrance of my pussy. Grinding my hips hard against his hand, I thrust his finger into my depths. Pope pulled his hand loose, only to drive his finger, plus a second one, back into my wanting sex. My hips shifted and rose, meeting each push of his hand. Water splashed everywhere as I desperately tried to quench the burning demand inside of me.

"I want to feel you come around my fingers. I want to feel you," Pope commanded.

His strokes became harder. His pinches along my nipple grew in intensity, causing me to helplessly thrash beneath his touch. Every nerve ending pulsated, electricity coursed to my womb as I allowed a cry to escape my mouth.

"Yes, baby. Come for me. Let yourself go." His demand was punctuated by another thrust of his finger.

I closed my eyes and allowed the pleasure to take over. Water splashed over the side of the bath as the satisfying feeling of completion overtook my body. My head fell back, and my hips convulsed as ecstasy exploded outward.

Before the last wave of the incredible orgasm rocked my body, I felt Pope's arms lift me out of the bath in one swift motion. The cool air heightened every touch, and my body hummed for more. He lay me down on a soft towel and quickly removed every item of his clothing that blocked his body and mine from uniting.

He sat on the ground and pulled me on top of his body. "Straddle me," he demanded.

I did as he asked, wrapping my legs on each side of his hips, pressing my wet knees against his warm and dry body. He grabbed his thick cock with his hand and directed it toward my entrance. "Put me in you. Bring yourself down on me."

I grabbed his dick, placed it at my wet pussy, and slid all the way down. My breath caught as my body struggled to adjust to his size. Any discomfort from the stretch was replaced with pure pleasure when Pope parted my pussy and found my clit. He continued the sensual caress as I rode his cock. Rising up slowly, and then driving down with a solid force. The slow pass of his fingers over my clit sent a shiver down my spine. The shiver turned to a heat that burned to my deepest core.

Pope's gaze, so full of confidence and strength, never left mine. He didn't hide the pleasure or passion he felt. He didn't hold back his groans as I thrust myself onto his cock, taking him deeper and deeper with every movement.

He pulled me against his chest and parted my lips with his. His kiss smothered my moans and captured my breath. He grabbed my hips with both hands and took control, increasing the pressure and building the speed, bringing me closer and closer to the sensation of pure bliss.

He moved his finger to the tight entrance of my backside and pressed firmly. My breathless gasp was rewarded with him pressing his finger all the way into my taboo depths.

I clenched around him as he pumped his finger in and out, releasing a hot desire from within me. Lust surged through me, my ass squirming... not away from the sensation but towards it as I leaned into his touch. Demanding more with my silent movements, he added a second finger past my tightly clenched rosebud. I couldn't help but press back against the invading fingers. I cried out his name as he worked his fingers inside the searing heat of my tight channel.

I saw him reach his hand and submerge it into a puddle on the floor, wetting his fingers with the oily lavender water from the bath. I bucked against his other fingers still in my ass, anxious of what was to come.

I tensed. Hearing the words of Vivian.

A good wife takes her husband's cock in the ass without complaint. A dutiful wife allows her ass to be fucked often.

"Relax, don't fight me." Pope's soothing words brought me back to reality.

I clenched on his fingers, struggling to ease my muscles and succumb to the intrusion. I moaned with a depraved sense of loss when he slowly withdrew his fingers from my ass and then groaned in pure pleasure when he switched hands, working his wet and oily fingers in and out, stretching my opening with each tantalizing pass.

Now we must prepare your tiny hole so that it is able to accept Pope's manhood.

Again, I fought back the thoughts of Vivian's perverse advice.

"Demi, don't. It's just us. No one else. Just you and me. Relax. Let me love you."

I closed my eyes and relaxed as Pope had instructed. I relaxed and enjoyed every little delicious taboo move.

The next time he pulled his fingers free, I was panting, desperate for his wicked digits to return. He ignored my, "Please, Pope," lifting me off his cock. He flipped me onto my stomach onto the cool tiled floor. "Stay still. Don't move," he commanded.

Hearing the sound of a bathroom drawer opening

and closing, then a snap of a lid, a shiver worked its way down my body. Pope was getting lubrication. I didn't need to see it to know what he had in mind next.

Moments later, his hand went between my thighs, resuming playing with my clit, reminding me of my out of control passion again. His hand returned to my behind and he began to spank lightly.

He bent over me and pressed his lips to my ear. "I'm going to fuck this ass."

I jerked as I felt Pope's cock nudge between the crevice in my behind. He spread my cheeks with his hands as he placed his hardness at my prepared opening. I cried out in pleasure as my tight hole eased open, stretching beyond what I thought possible.

"Pope, I'm not sure I can." Doubt, mixed with lust, clouded my mind.

"Trust me. I'm not going to hurt you."

"You're so big, I don't think I can take you." I whimpered as he pressed his bulging cockhead forward.

"Relax your muscles. Allow me in. I need to have you here. Breathe, Demi. Trust that this will feel good. It'll fucking hurt, but feel so good." His words were followed by kisses against my neck.

Pope moved a hand to my pussy and slid through the folds. Gently rubbing my clit, he pressed his cock past all resistance, burying his thickness all the way in. A ragged cry escaped my lips as a searing heat exploded deep within my anus.

Intense pleasure heightened with every move of his possession. "That's right. Just like that. Feel me take your ass."

Pope pressed two fingers into my pussy, moving in time with the thrusts of his cock in my tiny hole, letting me feel the pleasure of double penetration. His cock plunged harder and deeper inside of me as my moans echoed in the bathroom. Convulsive ripples ran from my anus to my pussy as an all-encompassing climax threatened to conquer me completely.

"Oh, God. Pope..."

"Press back into me. Drive my cock all the way into your ass. Make it hurt, allow the sting to make you come. Have the pain in your ass take away the pain in your heart. Fucking feel me!"

I did as he ordered. Shuddering, crying out, bucking against his hardness, I allowed the electricity to shoot through all parts of my body. I could only hold still as Pope grabbed my hips and forcibly thrust his cock hard one last time as he shot his seed deep within my forbidden channel.

No more pain.

No more darkness.

Pleasure. Long awaited pleasure.

20

The sound of Pope walking out on the deck to join me for our morning cup of coffee and fruit had my heart leap out of my chest. I had woken from a night of nightmares and hours of tossing and turning, and still couldn't shake the feeling. It still seemed impossible that Viv was dead. Vivian was dead.

"Did you get any sleep last night?" Pope asked as he sat down and picked up his mug of steaming brew.

I shook my head. "Barely, and when I did, I kept dreaming I was caught in that fire. I even had one dream where Vivian was holding me down against the floor, refusing to let me up as the shop burned around us. And then I had others where Maria and the baby were in the flames."

Pope reached across the tiny table and touched my arm tenderly. "It's all over. You're safe now. And I called a friend of mine back home and asked for him to check on Maria and Luis last night before you and I went to bed. He texted me this morning telling me they were safe and sound with no sign of Richard anywhere to be found."

I took a huge sigh of relief hearing the good news. "The rational part of me knows that. But then I can't help but feel as if any minute I'm going to hear that southern twang dictating how I should be a dutiful wife or else. I know she's gone, but I guess it hasn't really sunk in yet."

"The entire situation was fucked. It's to be expected that it's going to take time for you to get over all that happened. It's been an awful time."

I looked out onto the property as the morning sun shone brightly and saw the family of deer return for their breakfast grazing. It was like all the other mornings, yet today I was free. "It hasn't been all bad," I said softly as I sipped my coffee, almost in a trance as I watched the deer.

"No, it hasn't been all bad," Pope agreed.

I looked at him. "How are you doing? You lost your momma. Are you all right?"

He shrugged. "It hurts, but in many ways I had lost her years ago when Vivian entered our lives. She never was truly my mother after that. And when I went to prison, I had said my goodbyes to her then. I really hadn't planned on ever seeing her again. I thought she would have died before I was released. So I guess in many ways, I have already grieved her death."

I took a deep breath. "So, I suppose we have to face reality now. What to do now that I'm free."

"We do."

"I'm assuming Maria is worried about me." I shrugged. "Maybe not. She might have just assumed I skipped town. I'm sure my work and apartment did."

"Regardless, we need to get you back. It's a good day to fly. Weather's good."

A new sense of dread filled me. What if I didn't want to leave? What if I wanted to stay? Would that make me as insane as Vivian had been? What would Pope want? Was this really all over?

After a few minutes of silence and my mind going

crazy in thoughts, Pope asked, "Can we go for a walk?" His words broke me away from my onslaught of unanswered questions.

He stood up, set down his coffee and then mine. I reached for his hand and linked my fingers through his. I offered a smile as I stood, finding it impossible to give the man anything but. He made me happy. He made me smile.

Pope squeezed my fingers tightly between his as a shiver of delight went through me. The simplest of touches confirmed that Pope was the only man for me. No one had ever had such control over my emotions, my thoughts, and my body. Pulling me into his embrace, he just held me, his breath warm against my cheek. I didn't want to leave Pope. I didn't want this all to end, and the thought of my life returning to the way it was, shattered what was left of my soul.

After a few moments, he pulled back to look into my eyes and rested his palm against the side of my face. "We'll figure this all out."

I nodded. A glimmer of tears filled my eyes as the pain in my heart subsided. Pope reached out unexpectedly and gripped his hand around my waist. In one swift movement, he lifted me off the ground and pressed me hard against his chest.

Cradled so hard in his arms against him, I could feel his heart beating. His mouth came down powerfully on mine, his tongue plunging past my lips as if he were claiming me, possessing me as his. I clutched my arms around his neck as the world whirled around us, leaving nothing but overwhelming love.

I parted my lips, my hands desperately clinging to the fabric of the back of his shirt. Our tongues danced together as electric currents rippled through my body. My sex dampened at the sensation of Pope's body pressing against mine. My mind spiraled out of control with the knowledge of the erotic gratification we could bring each other. I melted into his embrace as he lowered me down to the wooden deck and very gently led me down the stairs.

We walked beside one another over the expansive land of the property. The sun began to climb above the horizon, casting a warm glow amongst the clouds. A cool breeze blew softly, causing my curls to escape from the loose bun I wore.

"I want to show you something," Pope said as he reached for my hand.

The soft caress made my pulse quicken. I wanted more of his touch.

As we reached the other side of the house, I squinted my eyes to block out the sunlight to make out the stunning picture before me. In nicely lined rows of five, stood at least twenty newly planted rose bushes.

I stared at the roses with bewilderment and awe. "These are beautiful! I know you both worked so hard on them. Viv would have loved seeing them start to bloom like they are right now."

Pope took a deep breath. "She wanted this to be the location of our wedding." He looked around and took in the blooming roses and sighed. "Ever since the day you were brought here—forced here—I've felt complete. You've changed and improved my life even though our world was in complete chaos. I hated that I wanted you. I despised the fact that a part of me was grateful that my mother had kidnapped you for me. It was so fucking wrong, yet I couldn't deny that fact. You were everything I ever wanted. That I needed. You've given me something I didn't even know was missing. You've given me love. You've given me light. And you've given me hope."

Pope walked us both so we were standing in the middle of all the rose bushes. He brushed his lips lightly against mine, giving such a delicate kiss.

"You were brought here against your will to marry me. But you deserved better. You deserve romance, and a fairytale story of the day your husband proposed. Not the nightmare my mother gave you. Gave the both of us. You deserved all the things a dutiful and proper *husband* would give *you*. I didn't give that to you... until now."

He smiled softly and got down on one knee. I began to cry at the sight of this strong, powerful man, on one bended knee, giving me the proposal I had fantasized about since being a little girl.

"I've fallen head over heels in love with you. And I would be a fucking fool to let you leave here not knowing how much I want you to stay in my life— by choice." My heart pounded so loud in my ears that I could barely hear him speak. "I want you in my life because I love you. Not because my mother is blackmailing us, but because I don't go a moment without thinking of you, without wanting you, and without loving you."

I wiped at the tears streaming down my face. A sob escaped my throat as I stared down at the most handsome man I had ever seen kneeling before me.

"Demi Wayne, will you please do me the honor of being my wife? Will you marry me?"

I threw my arms around his neck, knocking him to the ground. I straddled him on the grass, with the rose bushes all around, kissing him deeper and with more passion than I had ever done before.

Pope pulled away after a few moments of kissing me back with just as much fervor. "Is that a yes?"

I nodded and laughed alongside my tears. "Yes, yes! I love you! I love you! I love you!" I gave him a few more kisses and pulled back enough so I could see his entire face clearly. "I've never wanted anything more than you."

He laughed and kissed me lightly. "I love you. And I'll tell you those words every day of our lives."

My eyes burned and my heart swelled. "I want nothing more than to be your wife." I gave him a playful wink. "Your dutiful and obedient wife."

With a light chuckle and his eyes growing tender, Pope pressed his lips softly to mine. "I want you to remember this feeling you have right now. This massive amount of love we feel. Because as your husband, I vow to make sure you feel this every day, for the rest of our lives."

I leaned against Pope, content and at peace as I gazed up at him. "So what do we do now?"

Pope sat us both up, but still held me in his arms. "We head back home and tie up loose ends for you. Of course, check in on Maria and Luis for ourselves. See if your apartment is still there and your belongings."

I shook my head. "I don't want to return there. Can't we live here forever? I want to leave that dark part of my life behind me."

"Yes, we can, and I was hoping you would say that." He kissed the top of my head. "I want nothing more than to be here with you every single day."

Relief washed over me knowing that I didn't have to leave this wonderful haven I had somehow found a sense of home in for the first time. Viv had given me a home. She had given me love. For that, I would be forever grateful.

"I have something I need to give you," Pope said, reaching into his pocket and pulling out a letter. "My momma gave me this right before she died. She wanted you to read it."

My heart sunk when I saw the paper, remembering the other twisted letters from before. With shaky hands—reminding me of how Viv's hands also shook—I took the letter and began to read.

DEAR DEMI,

You were my friend. My real and true friend. I can never apologize enough for what I have done to you and for the pain I have caused. I am so ashamed. Even though I know you don't blame me, but rather blame my illness, because of the type of person you are, I still hope for forgiveness.

I love you, Demi. I know I have never said those words to you, but I do. I never had a daughter, but if I had, I would have wanted her to be just like you. And if I had lived to see the day you had married my son—regardless if it was because Vivian made you—I would have been so proud to be your momma.

I know I can't ask anything of you. I don't have that right. But please don't remember the worst of me. Please don't blame my son. Pope has been through so much, and I just hope you can show him the same amount of compassion that you showed me. Be his beacon in his thick darkness caused by me. Give him the light I so want him to have.

I don't know what is in store for you and my son. I can see love is there. Though I know many wounds are as well. Heal together. Maybe you won't become his bride, and you both will part ways when I am gone and Vivian has no more control. But if not... if you both decide to explore the love I see in your eyes, then allow me to give you some REAL motherly advice. A good wife is a wife who opens her heart and loves unconditionally. A dutiful wife is someone who returns the same love and passion that her dutiful husband gives her. And when you say your vows, remember each and every word. Read those vows when times grow dark. Live those vows. Become those vows.

I will be looking down on you both. Momma will be watching with love. Always.

~Viv

I WAS QUIET FOR A LONG TIME AFTER READING VIV'S goodbye to me, enjoying Pope's embrace, allowing the words in Viv's letter to sink in. Feeling Pope's breath dance with my hair. Hearing his heart beat against my cheek. I closed my eyes and luxuriated in the feeling of sincere, genuine, true love.

Finally, I whispered, "I take you. To honor and obey. Till death do us part. This is no longer my captive vow."

The End

ABOUT THE AUTHOR

Alta Hensley is a USA TODAY bestselling author of hot, dark and dirty romance. She is also an Amazon Top 100 bestselling author. Being a multi-published author in the romance genre, Alta is known for her dark, gritty alpha heroes, sometimes sweet love stories, hot eroticism, and engaging tales of the constant struggle between dominance and submission.

For More Information on Alta
www.altahensley.com
alta@altahensley.com

ALTA HENSLEY NEWSLETTER

ALTA HENSLEY'S HOT, DARK & DIRTY NEWS

Do you want to hear about all my upcoming releases? Get free books? Get gifts and swag from all my author friends as well as from me? If so, then sign up for my newsletter!

http://www.subscribepage.com/ion8g9

TOP SHELF SERIES

GET THE ENTIRE SERIES NOW!

TOP SHELF SERIES:

BASTARDS & WHISKEY

VILLAINS & VODKA

SCOUNDRELS & SCOTCH

DEVILS & RYE

ALSO BY ALTA HENSLEY

Devils & Rye

I didn't sell my soul to the devil...

He stole it.

Scoundrels & Scotch

I'll stop at nothing to own her.

I'm a collector of dolls.

All kinds of dolls.

Villains & Vodka

The name Harley Crow is one to be feared.

I am an assassin.

A killer.

The villain.

Bastards & Whiskey

Sipping on whiskey, smoking cigars, and conducting multi-million dollar deals in our own personal playground of indulgence, there isn't anything I can't have... and that includes HER. I can also have HER if I want.

And I want.

Captive Vow

I take you.

To honor and obey.

Till death do us part.

This is my solemn vow.

I am his.

Captive ever after...

Delicate Scars

I was delicate.

He was scarred.

But together...together we became delicate scars.

Snow & the Seven Huntsmen

This is no fairytale...

They've been sent to break me.

Not one, but seven.

They plan to steal my beauty, my innocence.

Seven Hunters to track me down and claim me as theirs.

I try to run, but it is hopeless.

They have caught me.

I am their prey, their prize, to do with as they please.

But I will capture something far more precious... the Huntsmen's hearts.

Red & the Wolves

This is no fairytale...

As the Blood Moon rises, I've been chosen.

Chosen to serve, to obey...to die...for no one survives their time with the Wolves.

As I am dressed in the ceremonial Red Hood, all I can think of is escape.

But there is no escape.

The lives of my village depend

on my submission to the accursed Wolves.

There are five of them.

Five men cursed to live as Wolves.

Cursed for generations, forced to protect my village from the dark forces.

But they demand a heavy price for their protection. Me.

Five against one...against me alone.

My only hope for survival is to tame the wolves...but submission is not in my nature.

Queen & the Kingsmen

This is no fairytale...

Captured and imprisoned.

They seek to break my curse by breaking me.

But I will not submit, no matter what tortures they have planned.

I am stronger then the Kingsmen.

Not just one man, but six.

For I am the powerful and feared evil queen.

My curse will stand.

For more of my books check out my Amazon Page!

http://amzn.to/2CTmeen

BASTARDS & WHISKEY

CHAPTER ONE

I stood before a table of assholes.

SIX FILTHY RICH, SMART AS FUCK, AND COMPLETE pricks sat around a circular African blackwood table. They each seemed annoyed they were even called to this meeting.

And why African blackwood—one of the most expensive woods in the world—a wood used to make instruments and one that had become nearly extinct because of mankind, you might ask? Why did we need such a luxurious table made of this wood in our office to conduct our meetings at?

Because we could.

Why did each of these assholes place their tumblers of high-end liquor over ice, dripping with condensation and leaving water rings on the delicate table?

Because we could.

We could do whatever the fuck we wanted.

We knew we were able to buy another table with an ease that made us cavalier toward possessions.

We were insanely rich, totally careless bastards. Each one of us.

Somewhere along the line, however, I had decided to become business partners with these ruthless men. On most days I felt as if I had made one hell of a wise financial decision pairing up with this motley bunch, and other days, I wondered how drunk I must have been on Macallan sherry oak whiskey to be fool enough to go in on this business idea. Had I known it was going to be so much work, I would've at the very least held out until someone treated me to The Balvenie 50-year-old single malt before agreeing to this bullshit.

And that's what this business had become.

Total and utter bullshit.

My ass didn't have time for this.

We owned *Spiked Roses*—an exclusive, membership only establishment in New Orleans where money or lineage was the only way in. It was for the gentlemen who owned everything and never heard the word no. Sipping on top shelf booze, smoking exotic cigars, and conducting multi-million dollar deals in our own personal playground of indulgence, there wasn't anything we couldn't have... and that had now become an issue. A big fucking, colossal problem that could make each one of us lose our asses in litigation and settlements.

"Listen, I don't want to be here either, fuckers," I began as I made eye contact with each man in the room. They were the powerful, royalty, the captains of industry, and the wealthiest fucks in the world.

They were also my friends, my business partners, and definitely some brutal and merciless shitheads who wouldn't be above doing whatever it took to protect what was theirs. *Whatever it took.*

"We just got hit with another lawsuit," I continued, looking down at the thick document in front of me, "and this one is a doozy." I looked back at the men who didn't seem bothered in the least. "And after we just got done paying out our asses for the last lawsuit..." I cleared my throat. "Make that the last couple of lawsuits. *Spiked Roses* is going to be in Chapter II before we even hit our one year anniversary."

One of the founding members—Prince Roman Cassian—looked around the table and said, "Last I checked, none of us were hurting for money. Since when are we afraid of some frivolous lawsuits and paying people off?" With his European accent, his charming smile, and his casual demeanor, I could see why women lined up for even a glimpse of the royal blood that surged through his cock. We'd even had to up security at the entrance because women were trying to sneak in with hopes of luring the sexy prince into their beds.

"We *have* paid people off. A lot! NOLA City Council is practically on our bi-weekly payroll right now. With two Councilmember-at-Large positions, and representatives in districts A through E, our payoffs are steep and plentiful. Plus, the mayor is breathing down our necks. He doesn't give a fuck what we do behind closed doors, but when it starts showing up in the courtrooms, he is losing his patience fast. So, something has to be done. And I don't know about any of you, but I didn't decide to open this club so some greedy bitch or asshole, who sees a payday in their future, can bleed my pocketbook dry," I said between clenched teeth.

I was pretty sure I wasn't the only founding member who would feel that way. But I also knew that since I handled all the legal matters of the business, it was very likely they all didn't truly grasp the severity and quantity in which the suits were being filed.

"Story of my life," Alec Sheldon said. Alec had made his fortune in oil and tobacco and was about as far away from a southern gentleman as you could get. He liked his sexual play dark and dirty, and he alone was one of the reasons we had to do something to protect *Spiked Roses* from future litigation. It was just a matter of time until his bedroom antics would land us in a multimillion-dollar sexual assault case. "Some little darlin' sues me if I even look at her wrong, let alone touch her." He took a long drink before adding, "It comes with the territory. We make money, and someone else wants to take it away. A hard lesson my pappy taught me was even if we don't hire a whore, we'll still pay for the sex one way or the other."

Some of the men nodded and snickered in agreement.

The dangerous Harley Crow was the next to chime

in. "And that's what we have you for, Mr. Kenneth Saxon. *You're* the vicious lawyer who destroys people in the courtroom. Am I correct? So go ahead and destroy." His snarky tone was not lost on me, but I wasn't going to say a thing. This son of a bitch was an assassin. No way to sugarcoat that fact. He killed people and made a shitload of money doing it. He was known as "The Crow", because if he showed up without warning, you knew bad things were about to happen. I was glad he was a friend and not an enemy, and I planned on keeping it that way. "Unless you want me to handle things my way," he added with an evil grin.

The other men all laughed and playfully told him to go for it. The Harley Crow way was the only way.

I fucking wished.

I released a sigh, feeling my frustration grow. "You fuckers won't be able to afford me for long." I reached down, lifted the thick document, and waved it for effect. "This one is for ten million dollars. And the one we just settled on was for nearly three million. The one before that was for five million. Shall I go on?"

I had finally gotten their attention. I saw grimaces, locked jaws, and stiffened spines.

I gave a smug nod. "That's right. And the fact of the matter is, that we are losing—or *would* lose if we didn't settle—because the women suing are within the law and have the right to have our heads on a stake. Our dirty ass members are doing the deeds these women claim, and all of you damn well know it."

"There are no rules at *Spiked Roses*. No one says no to a member," Victor Drayton pointed out as he sipped from his crystal tumbler. "Isn't that why we created this place? We were sick of all the stuffy rules and regulations of all those other membership clubs? Are you asking us to become just like them?" He shrugged. "We might as well close our doors then. I have no interest in being part of those blue blood men's clubs, and certainly don't want to own one."

Victor Drayton was the reason for the first lawsuit of 2.5 million dollars. He was a world-renowned gallery owner and art collector, but he also was known in the dark shadows of *Spiked Roses* for *Drayton's Dolls*. He collected "dolls" which involved naked women being painted and then hung on display. Sounded normal and consensual enough, but based on the claim made by one of the "dolls" who sued us, it didn't stop with just being painted as art for one of his galleries. The kinky descriptions of the art room in the deposition even had my filthy ass doing a double take.

I dipped my index finger between the knot of my silk tie and the cotton of my shirt to loosen the restriction a bit. I prepared myself for what I was about to propose. All eyes were on me; I had gotten their attention when I mentioned the loss of millions, but now they were looking for a solution.

"I'm not asking that we change the expectations of the members. You are right, Victor. We opened *Spiked Roses* because conventional isn't a word to describe any of us. I'm not saying we change the men, but we need to change the women and how we go about things."

I paused so my words could sink in. I took hold of my glass of whiskey and sipped it before continuing, taking the time to inhale the aroma of the aged-to-perfection liquid.

"The first thing we are going to do is clean house. All new staff," I began. "We aren't running a whore house, a drug den, or a strip club. And if you look around and really take stock, that's what's been happening. We have enough cocaine, heroin, and even meth being passed around in dark corners to have all our asses sent to prison for a very long time."

"Ah come on, man. Cleaning house? That's harsh," Prince Roman interjected. "They aren't all bad or on drugs."

"Agreed. They aren't all bad. But those who aren't fully fucked up end up getting chosen to become arm candy by one of our members. They become the flavor of the month—or week—which means that our fucking staffing needs are a disaster. Those women don't show up for work because they are fucking some count on his yacht," I said as I finally took the seat at the head of the table.

"He's right," Matthew Price agreed. "We are rarely fully staffed lately, and the members are starting to complain about the speed of getting their drinks. Hell, we haven't had a cigar girl working the floor in days. It's not good business, gentlemen. Fuck all the lawsuits. They don't matter if we have a shitty place to come to."

Finally, I had someone else stepping up and speaking the harsh truths, and probably the best person in the room to do so. Matthew Price was a Captain of Industry in every way. He was the CEO and owner of Price Enterprises, and known for conquering his enemies by destroying their business value and then swooping in for the kill and buying up what was left. He was the king of the jungle, and a predator who couldn't be stopped.

"I agree with Kenneth," Matthew continued. "It's time to clean house and start fresh. We also need a housemother of some sort. Someone to guarantee our staff follow the strict guidelines that we need to set. And we need fucking uniforms. I'm sick of seeing an array of fashion out on the floor. Just saying 'sexy' isn't enough. We need to set the parameters of what sexy is."

"Like a madam?" Alec asked. "I thought we wanted to get *away* from the image of running a whore house."

"We can polish the title up however we want to make it not appear as a madam. Maybe hire a man to do the job for all I care." Matthew paused as if considering his words. "A gay man so we know he won't fuck them in the back room."

"A daddy. I like it," Alec said with a wicked smile. "A strict daddy to keep them all in line."

"I may have the perfect person for the job," Lennon Wolf chimed in. Lennon ran with some of the artsy and most eccentric people out of all of us. The type of people who owned monkeys or zebras and kept them in their backyard. It was impossible to show up at a fancy party and not see Lennon Wolf standing with a martini glass in his hands. He was the life of the party, and no party was complete without his presence. Known for gaining his wealth by being an art and jewelry thief, he was also known for never stealing from his friends. So, if you had valuable art and jewels, it was crucial to become friends with the man. Unless you wanted your rare Picasso to turn up missing that is. "His name is Tennessee Charles, and last I heard, his own sugar daddy just cut him off, so he'll be looking for employment. But I know Tennessee, and he will have the women marching to his orders in a way that only that man can do."

"Good," Matthew said with a nod. "Bring him in. We need to start there. But make sure he's a strict and mean motherfucker, because it's time that *Spiked Roses* gets the reputation of not fucking around with the staff. No nonsense. We want people to be afraid if they'll keep their jobs on a nightly basis. Mandatory drug tests and STD checks as well. I'm sick of coked out women working the floor."

Since it appeared everyone in the room was now open to some reshaping of our original vision, I decided to broach the biggest change I wanted to see happen. "From now on, I would like to see contracts come into play. If any of our members—and that includes the founding members sitting here—want to fuck any of the staff, then they need to both sign a contract. In a nutshell, the contract states that both parties are openly and freely engaging in a sexual relationship. That for the length of the contract, the male owns the female. He has bought her, and she has allowed it. If you fuck her, you buy her. Simple."

I could see the looks of shock and confusion on the men's faces, so I quickly continued before any of them had a chance to say a word.

"Both parties can end the contract at any time. But if the member ends the contract, there is a fee to the female staff for doing so. A severance package of sorts. It protects the female because from now on, if she signs the contract, she will no longer be employed with *Spiked Roses*. So she will need a hefty compensation for when the contract ends." I paused just long enough to take a drink and try to organize my thoughts better to fully explain the contract so it wouldn't be confusing to someone who was not an attorney. "The reality is that we know all the relationships end eventually. The members grow tired of their arm candy and want someone new. The women go into it thinking they found their sugar daddy, and when it comes to a crashing halt, they get pissed and many want to sue. But they sue because they feel cheated somehow. Cheated of their payday. So, we are going to put in the contract that they do indeed get paid when the relationship ends. Now, if the woman ends the contract, that is on her. No payment. The man doesn't owe her anything. And if we have a position open, she can always reapply, but there are no promises that her job will be held for her. Basically, gentlemen, I'm trying to protect our asses. To fuck one of our girls, you have to buy her first. Arm candy, or a quick fuck, or even a long term relationship is not free anymore. If you meet her at *Spiked Roses*, and if you want more than just a pretty sight to look at, then you need to sign on the dotted line."

"How much?" Prince Roman asked. "How much will we be expected to pay if we end things after a little fun?"

"Depends on the negotiations," I answered. "Standard contract is one year's salary at *Spiked Roses*. But every contract can be negotiated."

"And you think members and the staff will actually sign this?" Harley Crow asked.

"They have to if they want more. No one has to sign a thing, but then they need to not fuck. Black and white. If you want to fuck her, you have to buy her. And if you want to fuck him, you have to be willing to be bought. It protects both parties. The man can't get sued for sexual harassment or assault, and the female doesn't get left in the dust when the man gets bored. And like I said, the contract can last as long or as short as both parties want. It can be for just one night, or it can be for months. No more of that boyfriend/girlfriend shit here. It always backfires and then *Spiked Roses* somehow gets sued."

"I like it," Matthew said with a nod. "The contract proves the woman is giving consent."

"Yes," I said. "Plus, we can add any line items that may be a bit extraordinary like Victor expects with his *dolls*."

Victor smiled and lifted his drink in a mock cheer. "I like your thinking, my friend."

"And those sex parties that we have all been talking about hosting lately in The Tasting Room," I said which had all of their eyes light up. "We can move forward with those now. The women will go into each sex party with clear expectations, the members will also know the rules, and official contracts will be written for each party. The difference with the sex parties, however, is that the staff won't lose their jobs if they engage in a contract in The Tasting Room. That will be considered as part of their job—if they want to attend. No mandate will be set that any female *has* to attend. The Tasting Room is where the business happens, and once a contract is signed, the members can use one of our hotel rooms, or take the woman home. If it is just one night of sex, the contract will say so. If it's more, then we will stipulate that as well. We are putting consent on paper, gentlemen. Putting it in writing so we don't get fucked up the ass in litigation. And just for fun, and to add some ceremonial aspect to it, I was thinking we could have both parties prick their finger and seal it with blood."

"I like," Harley Crow said. "Anything with blood is a winner in my book."

"And you don't think this is prostitution? You are saying you want our members to buy the women," Alec said with skepticism. "That's illegal if you ask me, Mr. Lawyer."

"No," I replied quickly. "The members are asked to pay when the sex ends. When they are done and want to end the contract. The sex is free, but ending it is not. The Tasting Room is different, and yes, I guess you could call it prostitution, or you can call it arranged dating. But no one is being forced to enter that room." I released a large sigh. "I'm not saying this idea of the contract is completely on the up and up. Hell, it won't even hold up in a court of law. But it's better than what we have now. It at least makes it very clear what is expected by both parties. If, by some chance, we do land in court again—which is very likely—when we pay off the judges, we can at least put their minds at ease that the entire situation was consensual. Or at least as close as we could get to it." I looked down at the document before me. "The latest suit is because Jackson Latham brought one of our staff to his little house of horrors, tied her up for three days, and sexually 'tortured' her as the claimant states. But we all know that Jackson is known for his kidnapping kink, and we also know Jessica James knew of that kink and she and Jackson had been fucking around for weeks. But this was her payday, and now this poor fucker is going to have to pay out the ass and pray to God he doesn't have criminal charges placed against him because it's her word against his. He claims consent; she claims kidnapping. If they both had signed a contract—with a little stamp of blood from both parties for pizzazz—where it states what his kink is and his expectations, then he wouldn't be in this position, and *Spiked Roses* wouldn't be a codefendant in this really fucking expensive lawsuit. We have legal issues out our ass, so much so, that I have had to hire a legal team to help me out."

"Not all women are guilty of looking for that payday you mention," Prince Roman argued.

"I know that," I said with a nod. "And it has also become our job to protect the women who work for us. This does that. Often women get fooled or blinded by all the promises of love and care. And when they let their guards down, they ultimately get screwed. I don't know about you, gentlemen, but I have yet to hear of a love story emerging from *Spiked Roses*. So, with this contract, it protects their interest. Black and white. And every woman hired will see this contract upon employment. They never have to sign one if they don't want to. Never. Unless, of course, they want to fuck a member of *Spiked Roses* or attend one of the tastings. Then, it is mandatory. Mandatory for our members too. If they want to fuck, or have fucked one of our staff and we find out, they must sign a contract or forfeit their membership and all fees associated with it."

"But do we really need to clean house?" Prince Roman asked. "I guess I'm not a heartless fucker like all of you," he said with his trademark charming grin.

"It's setting the stage," Matthew added. "We have to build an unbending reputation starting now. It's better to start over and from the beginning than to expect people to change. No one likes change. And right now, the women are talking. They know how much others are getting as a payday in the settlements and want a part of that as well. So, we need to start fresh. Show that we are taking control, and this suing shit is about to come to a screeching halt. Fast."

Matthew was clearly on my side, but the others didn't seem as convinced.

I stood up like I had started the meeting and like I always did in court when I really wanted to drive the point home, and said, "Gentlemen, please pull out your wallets and place whatever cash you have in the center of the table." When no one immediately did as I asked, I added, "Come on, you stingy bastards, humor me and do it."

Each man begrudgingly did as I asked as they reached into their pockets. Hundreds of dollars were placed by each man, and, in some cases, thousands.

"Matthew, do you mind counting that up for me?" I asked.

Matthew took hold of the cash and quickly counted. "Nine thousand and fifty dollars."

I nodded and then reached over to the intercom and hit the button, waiting for the secretary to answer.

"Yes, sir?" came a soft voice on the other end.

"Lena, can you come in here please?" I asked.

A few moments later, Lena came in and stood by the door, looking nervous as she scanned the room and saw all the founding members sitting around the table. She wore a tiny black dress that accentuated every delicious curve of her body, black pumps that tightened the firm muscles of her legs, and her long black hair flowed freely down her back. She had the look of a beautiful baroque goddess, and I knew by a quick glance at every man in the room, that she was one of the most fuckable women any of us had seen in a long time. My cock twitched at the thought of having it buried deep inside her while all the men watched on with envy.

"Lena, did you get a response from the new HR manager who we offered the job to yesterday?"

She diverted her eyes from the staring men and looked at me directly. "Yes, sir. He said he will start with the new hiring tomorrow first thing. I also told him you or one of the founding members would be overseeing the interviews."

I nodded. "Very good, thank you." I motioned for her to go ahead and leave, which she did quickly without saying another word.

Lennon Wolf whistled and leaned back in his chair. "Woo, she is a looker indeed."

I smiled. "That she is. I can see you all agree." It was obvious on each man's face. "It's clear you all want to fuck her. I sure as hell do. So, who here is prepared to buy her and sign that contract I mentioned? Right now. Buy her so you can fuck her within the hour. Anyone?"

I paused and looked around, seeing that not one man was jumping up and saying yes.

"No one? No one wants to sign the contract?" When no one answered, I added, "Good. Do you see, gentlemen? This will help keep our members in check. Many will sign the contract because we are all dirty bastards, but it will make the business man come out in all of us and at least make us pause and think about our actions. It will hold us accountable. It will also make the parties in The Tasting Room more profitable, because those contracts are short term and don't require the same commitment."

I buzzed Lena back in and waited.

"Yes, sir?" she said with more confidence this time as she entered the room.

"Lena, you are fired. *Spiked Roses* is terminating all current employees effective immediately." I pointed to the large pile of cash in the middle of the table. "Take what's there. It's yours. Consider it your severance package."

Tears filled the poor girl's eyes and her lip began to quiver.

"Nothing against you, Lena. But *Spiked Roses* is about to be reborn."

SNOW & THE SEVEN HUNTSMEN

CHAPTER ONE

I t was barely a sound.

The soft scrape of a boot on the floor. The rub of a shoulder against the stone wall. A muffled cough.

I was awake in an instant. Something was different. There was a tension in the air.

Throwing my covers aside, I shivered when my feet touched the icy flagstone floor. Creeping over to the high-arched windows, I parted the brocade curtains just enough to peek out. All was quiet and still. The newly fallen snow lay undisturbed, glistening and sparkling in the moonlight.

Perhaps I had imagined it?

Another sound.

This one just beyond my bedroom door.

A horrible calm settled over me as if a long anticipated storm had finally broken. I had been waiting for this day. Dreading it.

My stepmother had finally sent someone to kill me.

With my only escape route now blocked to me, I had to think fast. Pushing open the heavy curtains, I placed my hands on the black ebony frame. I once again looked over the winter scene below, the peace of a winter's eve now destroyed. My bedroom was far too high to risk a jump, but perhaps I could climb out onto the ledge and make my way to the stone balustrade of the room next door.

There was the screech of metal against metal. The scrape of a key. They were unlocking my door.

Running across the room, I picked up the small wooden spindle chair by the perpetually cold fireplace. It was one of the few pieces of furniture I was allowed in my sparse prison. Hefting it high, I raced back to the window. I hesitated. The moment I broke the window, there would be no turning back. I would have to run and keep running. I squeezed my eyes shut and smashed the chair against the glass with all my might. It shattered, sending sharp shards skittering across the floor. Grabbing the blanket off my bed, I placed it over the jagged pieces. Stepping up to the window, I tossed the remnants of the bedcovers over the sill, cutting my finger in the process. I watched in horrid fascination as three warm, crimson spots of blood fell upon the snow on the ledge, melting it.

As I gingerly stepped onto the sill, the bedroom door opened. A bitter wind cut through the threadbare fabric of my nightgown as remnants of the broken window sliced into my bare feet. With a cry, I moved onto the ledge, quickly turning to grasp the chilled stone.

Morbid curiosity getting the better of me, I peered back into the interior of my room. Looking over my shoulder, I saw three men enter, moonlight illuminating them. The brawn and bulk of their size belied their almost silent entry.

So similar they could be brothers, each was tall with broad shoulders and a harsh angular face. They wore animal skins and furs. Trophies of their past kills.

Huntsmen.

Spurred on by their fearsome looks, I dug my fingernails into the stone façade and tried to slide my foot to the right. It slipped on the ice-covered ledge. My cry of alarm echoed across the still forest, sending sleeping birds into flight.

"Well, the lass has spirit. I will give her that," said one of the men happily, a note of appreciation in his dark voice.

"Good. This would be no fun if she didn't have some fight in her," said another while clapping the first on the shoulder.

"There is no point in running. We will only hunt you down," said the third to me.

"Why have you come?" I asked.

"You know why."

I could feel all three men assessing me. No doubt, the bright moonlight was shining through my gown, leaving little to their lascivious imaginations. Was I to be used for their pleasure before they killed me? I cast a look over my shoulder to the drifts below. I could hear new voices outside, their conversation carrying across the hushed midnight landscape. More men.

"Are you going to be a good girl and come along quietly?" asked the first. With his feet planted and his arms crossed over his massive chest, he made for a foreboding sight.

"I could scream," I warned. The words came out weak and trembling as my teeth had begun to chatter from the cold.

"And no one would come to your aid."

The truth of their words sent the air rushing from my lungs. I was completely alone. The wretched irony was this conversation with my killers was the first a human being had spoken to me in years. My stepmother had ordered the servants and villagers to ignore my presence and never to speak to me almost from the moment my father had drawn his last breath. I had been wrapped in a blanket of silence and solitude for as long as I could remember.

I could feel the tears pool in my eyes. As they dropped, they froze on my chilled cheeks. "You could let me go," I whispered.

"No. We can't. You are a prize we have fought long and hard to claim. You belong to us now," explained the third man.

My brow wrinkled at his words. "You're not here to kill me?"

A bark of laughter came from all three men.

The first one answered for the group. "You may trust us in this, lass. The very last thing we plan to do is kill you."

"Enough talk," ground out the second grumpily. "The others are waiting below."

He stepped before me. Laying a hand on my chest, he pushed.

Flailing, my outstretched hands scrambled for some kind of purchase but only met with air. The sound of rushing wind tormented me as I fell backwards into nothingness. My scream lost. What was only an instant felt like an eternity.

Then...instead of the cold embrace of death, I felt warmth.

I was held in a pair of strong arms. The feel of soft fur caressed my cheek. He smelled of pine and whiskey. I looked up into his bearded face, surprised when he gave me a wink.

"Well, men. It looks like I have caught some falling Snow."

I was surrounded by hearty laughter.

With a start, I craned my neck around. Three large burly men stared back at me with interest. Another four men.

Seven in total.

With a screech, I twisted and turned my body, trying to break free. The man who held me easily tossed me over his shoulder. I felt the heat of his large hand on the undercurve of my ass.

"You bastard!" I yelled. "Get your hands off me!"

I had a brief moment of satisfaction when I felt his hand move away. Then there was a burst of raw pain. His open palm had struck my right buttock. The thin fabric of my gown did not keep the prickling hot needles from racing over my chilled skin.

Shock kept me immobile.

One of the other men circled round my captor's back. Grabbing my dark, ebony hair, he forced my head up. I winced at the twinge of pain.

Addressing the assembled men, he said, "Let's get our new prize home so we can really begin her punishment."

I opened my mouth to scream, but he shoved a gag between my red lips, tying it tightly behind my head.

Once upon a time, I was a princess named Snow White...now, I am the captive prize of seven huntsmen.

Made in the USA
Las Vegas, NV
29 December 2020